"Pleas___
know why you're flirting with Scarlett."

"Well, JD sent me down to help you Mel, but—this is really hard—the way I'm supposed to help is that I'm supposed to start dating Scarlett."

"But . . . but you can't!" Melody exploded, tears in her eyes. "You just can't!"

He hasn't even kissed me yet, Melody thought. *JD, how could you do this to me?*

Other Avon Flare Books in the
TEEN ANGELS *Series by*
Cherie Bennett

HEAVEN CAN'T WAIT
LOVE NEVER DIES

TEEN ANGELS
#3

Angel Kisses

Cherie Bennett

AN AVON  FLARE BOOK

TEEN ANGELS #3: ANGEL KISSES is an original publication of Avon Books. This work has never before appeared in book form.

AVON BOOKS
A division of
The Hearst Corporation
1350 Avenue of the Americas
New York, New York 10019

Copyright © 1996 by Cherie Bennett and Jeff Gottesfeld
Published by arrangement with the authors
Library of Congress Catalog Card Number: 95-95059
ISBN: 0-380-78249-9
RL: 6.7

First Avon Flare Printing: March 1996

AVON FLARE TRADEMARK REG. U.S. PAT. OFF. AND IN OTHER COUNTRIES, MARCA REGISTRADA, HECHO EN U.S.A.

Printed in the U.S.A.

RA   10 9 8 7 6 5 4 3 2 1

To the tens of thousands of teens around the world who have written to us—you are the greatest

One

"I have a zit, my hair looks like dogmeat, and I'm expecting my period," Cisco McCaine complained to her roommates, Melody Monroe and Nicole Van Owen, as she peered at her reflection in a tiny mirror propped up on her desk. "Let's face it, I look like some ole thing the cat dragged in," she drawled. "And I don't even want to go to this stupid dance, anyway."

"But it's our first dance since we've been in Teen Heaven!" Melody pointed out in her breathy, child-like voice. "I think it will be so much fun!" She closed her eyes for a moment and thought about Chaz Denton. *He's so wonderful,* Melody thought blissfully. *And he cares about the real me, not just what I look like.*

"You're all excited because you're going with Chaz," Cisco pointed out.

"That's true," Melody admitted shyly.

Cisco looked over at Nicole, who was sticking little pearl studs in her ears. "And you're going with that hunka-hunka burnin' love, Jake. I am solo, with zits and disgusting hair."

1

"You could have had a date if you wanted a date," Nicole said, in her usual logical fashion. "You didn't want one."

"I'm not ready," Cisco admitted, frowning into the mirror.

"Is it Shayne?" Melody asked sympathetically.

Shayne Stone had been Cisco's first Earth assignment. He was a musician who had been slowly committing suicide with fame, alcohol, and drugs. Cisco had shown Shayne the trouble he was headed for and in the process they'd fallen in love. And when Cisco had to return to Teen Heaven, it had broken her heart.

"Partly," Cisco said with a sigh. "And partly . . . I just don't want to have a boyfriend right now. When I was still alive I thought I had to have a boyfriend or I would just die. Now, was that stupid, or what?"

"I was always like that, too," Melody said. "I must have had a hundred boyfriends!"

"Well, Jake is my first," Nicole admitted. "I never really had a boyfriend on Earth, so I can't relate."

"It wasn't always so wonderful," Melody said. "When I think back . . . I used to fall for a guy just because he was nice to me and told me I was beautiful!"

"But you *are* beautiful, Melody," Nicole pointed out. "I'm sure you've always had guys falling all over you."

"But that doesn't have anything to do with real love," Melody said earnestly. "Every time I had a new boyfriend I thought it would be different, that he would be the guy who would really love me, but I was wrong. Mostly they just wanted . . . you know."

"See, this just bites my angelic butt—" Cisco began. "See how ridiculous girls act? Do you think boys

2

go around thinking they're nothing if they don't have a girlfriend?''

"Girls, girls!" cried out a girl with shining blonde curls, huge blue eyes, and wearing braces on her teeth, who bounded into the room. "I just had to come get your opinion on my outfit!"

"Don't you believe in knocking, Celeste?" Cisco asked, eyeing the blonde girl with distaste.

Celeste Durkey was the class suck-up. She also was certain she knew everything about everything, and she made sure everyone else knew she knew it. She had been living at the opposite end of the hall from Melody, Cisco, and Nicole, but her roommate had literally begged Free, their housemother, to move her, and now Celeste was right next door, in the only single in the dorm.

She was utterly obnoxious, and no one could stand her.

Which means that you can be obnoxious and still become a Teen Angel, I guess, Melody thought to herself.

It still amazed Melody to realize that she herself was a Teen Angel, that she actually was dead. Dead. It was so final—and so scary.

She thought back to her life when she'd still been alive, an eighteen-year-old in Detroit, Michigan. Her whole life people had told her that she looked and sounded like Marilyn Monroe. People thought she was faking it, but Melody was just being herself.

After her parents split up when she was ten, things had been hard for her mom, Melody, and her younger brother and sister. Her mom's earnings as a waitress had barely made ends meet, and her father had disappeared without a trace.

3

When Melody was twelve, she'd gotten her first job as a print model, and ever since then she'd been the major breadwinner in the family. Her mother was constantly on her about her looks—don't get a pimple, get enough sleep, and, most of all, don't ever, ever gain an ounce—because if Melody didn't look good, the family didn't eat. Eventually her mother had quit her job as a waitress—to manage Melody's "career," she said.

Melody was always a sucker for good-looking, sweet-talking guys, just like her mother. Melody's fantasy was that the right guy would come along and carry her off to a wonderful life. They would get married, she'd have lots of animals and live on a farm somewhere; she'd have babies and bake bread and live happily ever after.

Her mother thought she was crazy.

And because everyone thought that being a model was so wonderful, Melody hardly every confessed her secret yearnings to anyone. But the truth of the matter was that she hated modeling, and she hated never being able to eat desserts, always going hungry just so she could remain thin. She didn't have any aspirations to become an actress, even though her mother was certain that Melody was going to become a big star and make the family rich.

Yet Melody never had enough courage to stand up for herself.

So when her latest boyfriend, a drop-dead gorgeous male model named Buddy had insisted that he drive the car home from their date after they both modeled at the auto show, even though Melody knew for certain that Buddy was drunk, she let him drive.

Buddy crashed the car.

He lived, she died. The end.

Or not, depending upon how you looked at it, because Melody had landed in Teen Heaven, where teens who die end up when they still have lessons of life to learn.

And it's just like Earth, Melody thought ruefully, high school and all! The only difference is that except for the house parents in the dorms and the teachers, there are no adults.

And because she had died at exactly the same time as Cisco and Nicole, the three of them had become roommates at one of the Teen Heaven dorms. Now they were also best friends.

And we're so different, Melody thought with a smile. Cisco McCaine is a smart, tough, funny girl from a tiny town in Tennessee. She used to have a drinking problem, but she went to rehab, and it changed her life.

She no longer wanted to hang out with the cool crowd and get loaded. She thought her longtime boyfriend would understand how she felt, but it turned out that he didn't. In fact, he cheated on her when she was in rehab. When Cisco found out, she was so angry that she went for an out-of-control ride on her motorcycle without a helmet.

It was the last reckless thing she would ever do.

And smart, logical Nicole Van Owen, with her perfect long, straight red hair and impeccable manner, was a rich girl from Princeton, New Jersey. She had always lived up to her parents' extremely stringent expectations for her, until the day she found out that she'd only received 950 on her SATs. That score would never get her into Princeton, and not going to Princeton, in Nicole's family, would have been a terrible disgrace.

So she took an overdose of sleeping pills rather than face her parents, Melody recalled. She didn't really want to die, she just didn't want to face her parents.

We all made some stupid decisions, Melody thought with a sigh. But all three of us thought we'd live forever. It just never occurred to any of us that we could actually die.

Teen Heaven, Melody had learned, was run by a guy named JD, who looked exactly like James Dean, a movie star from the fifties. JD had explained to Melody, Cisco, and Nicole how Teen Heaven worked.

The Big Guy (and everyone knew who *that* was!) would send a Teen Angel down to Earth on an assignment, where he or she would try to influence a teen in trouble to make positive changes in his or her life. If the mission succeeded, that Teen Angel would earn angel points, and when he or she earned enough points, it would be time for Ultimate Heaven, which JD said was "so cool you couldn't even envision such coolness."

Of course, JD told them, they'd have no special unearthly powers Down Below. "Knowledge is power," he'd said.

"Why should I knock?" Celeste was asking. "We're all girls. Right, Melody?"

Melody was pulled from her thoughts by Celeste's overly perky voice. "Oh, right," she agreed.

Celeste gave Melody a huge grin. She always seemed to be out to impress Melody because she thought Melody was the prettiest girl in Teen Heaven.

"I'm so glad that Free transferred me to the room next to the three of you!" Celeste bubbled on enthusiastically. "I baked her a double batch of butterscotch chip cookies to thank her! And of course I wrote her a thank-you note, too. I also made a copy of the thank-you note for my files, in case she ever claims that she didn't get it.''

Celeste twirled around. ''So, what do you think, Melody?''

Melody eyed Celeste's outfit, which was quite extraordinary. She had on a short, full pink skirt with a white crinoline petticoat underneath, which made the skirt stand out from her body as if it had a life of its own. With it she wore a fuzzy pink sweater covered with tiny pink and white bows, and she wore a matching oversized pink bow in her blonde curls.

''It's . . . interesting,'' Melody said, since she could never bear to hurt anyone's feelings.

''You look like Little Bo Peep on acid,'' Cisco said bluntly.

Celeste turned on her. ''That wasn't funny.''

''Yes it was,'' Cisco replied, scrutinizing her own face in the mirror again.

Celeste came around to peer closely at Cisco. ''You have a humungous zit on your chin,'' she reported.

''Celeste, how can I put this so I won't hurt your feelings?'' Cisco mused. ''You annoy me and I wish you would disappear?''

Celeste wandered toward the door. ''So, I suppose the three of you are going over to the dance together, huh?''

''We're going in Nicole's car,'' Melody said. All the Teen Angels had their own cars—mostly vintage convertible Mustangs in their favorite color. ''We're meeting Chaz and Jake there.''

''Oh,'' Celeste said, kicking at the floor with her patent leather Mary Jane shoes. ''I was going to drive myself . . .'' She looked over at Melody. ''But I wouldn't mind going with you guys.''

Cisco shot Melody a look that said, ''don't you

dare invite her," and Nicole also gave her a stern look, but Melody couldn't stand to see how left out Celeste felt.

"I think it would be okay for you to come with us," Melody said with a little shrug of apology to her friends.

"Oh, goody, goody, goody!" Celeste squealed. "I *knew* you wanted me to come with you! I'll meet you guys downstairs in ten minutes. Okay? Bye!" She then raced out the door.

"How *could* you?" Nicole asked Melody.

"I'm sorry," Melody apologized. "I just couldn't say no!"

"You let everyone walk all over you, girl," Cisco drawled. "Where's your self-respect?"

"I know I should stand up for myself, but it's hard," Melody said with a sigh. She sat down on her bed, picked up her white kitten, Ruffy, and began to stroke her fur. "I'm always worried that I'm going to hurt someone's feelings."

"It's okay, Mel," Nicole said, as she went to the closet to pull out her outfit for the dance. "You're just a kind person."

"Where I come from we call it being a wuss," Cisco snapped. She got up from her desk and walked over to her bed, where she eyed the outfit she'd laid out.

"You're in a foul mood," Nicole said. She slipped her conservative navy-blue dress with white piping over her head and smoothed it down.

"I know, I'm hateful," Cisco agreed. "Ignore me." She pulled off her jeans and T-shirt and pulled on the black miniskirt, tiny white shirt, and black suspenders that she'd laid out earlier.

Melody tried to see her own outfit in the tiny mirror

on the desk. She had on a short white skirt that flared at the hemline and a white sweater that bared an inch of her stomach. "Why can't we get some decent mirrors in here?" she asked, turning this way and that to try and catch sight of her whole reflection.

"Don't worry," Nicole said, smoothing down her dress. "You look absolutely perfect."

Melody put her hands on her stomach. "You don't think I look fat?"

"Yes, you're a pig," Cisco said sarcastically. "I don't know how you even live with yourself."

"My stomach is kind of poofing out," Melody said with a frown.

"Oh, you angels!" Celeste said in a singsongy voice from the doorway. "I'm all ready!"

"You told us you were meeting us downstairs," Nicole reminded her.

"I just stopped here first to tell you that I'm heading downstairs now," Celeste reported. She eyed Cisco. "Your outfit is kind of slutty looking. No offense."

"From you, Celeste, I take that as a compliment," Cisco drawled.

"Well, a little constructive criticism never hurt anyone!" Celeste pointed out. "Anyway, since we're all going to the dance together, we'll all hang out there together, right? Except when we're dancing, of course. So, I'll be downstairs!"

As soon as Celeste left Nicole and Cisco gave Melody evil looks.

"Okay, I shouldn't have invited her to come with us," Melody admitted. "I'll learn to say no. Really, I will!"

"Yo, ladies," a voice called from the doorway.

It was JD, leaning against the doorframe. He had

on a worn leather jacket and his usual jeans, and he was his usual gorgeous self.

"Hi, JD," Melody said, reaching for the perfume bottle on the dresser.

"May I say that the three of you are looking extremely lovely," JD said.

"You may," Nicole replied.

Melody smiled at Nicole. Nicole had had the world's biggest crush on JD, until she'd fallen for Jake.

"Have a blast at the dance tonight," JD said.

"Aren't you coming?" Cisco asked.

"I have a date with a certain someone," JD explained.

"A certain someone named Natalie?" Cisco asked innocently.

She was refering to Natalie Wood, who the girls were pretty sure JD was seeing. Not that he'd ever admit it, any more than he'd admit that he really was James Dean.

"Hey, I don't kiss and tell, babe," JD said breezily. He turned to Melody. "So, listen, I just wanted to let you know that tonight's the night."

"The night for what?" Melody asked wide-eyed.

JD raised his eyebrows. "What have you been waiting for?"

And then it dawned on her. "My first Earth assignment?" she asked with excitement.

"Bingo!" JD said. "After the dance, you'll find your dossier on your desk, waiting for you."

Suddenly Melody felt nervous. Cisco and Nicole had both already had their first Earth assignments, and they both had done so well. *What if I'm the only one who messes up*? she worried. "JD, can you tell me a little about my assignment?"

"You'll know soon enough, babe," JD assured her. "Just go have fun tonight and forget about it 'til later."

"But—" she began.

"Hey, 'Never hurry, never worry,' that's what I always say," JD said, giving them his favorite quote from his favorite book, *Charlotte's Web*.

"I'm going to be nervous all night now," Melody admitted. "Knowing I'm going soon, but not knowing anything about it, will drive me crazy with anxiety!"

JD sighed. "You girls are so intense!" He thought a moment. "Okay, I'll give you a little hint. What's something you missed out on when you were on Earth?"

"Bad hair days?" Cisco guessed.

"Melody knows," JD said, staring at Melody. "Something you didn't really get to do because you were so busy working as a model."

"Well," Melody said slowly, "I didn't really get to go to high school my senior year. Not very much, anyway . . ."

"Bingo again!" JD said.

"I'm going back to high school on Earth?" Melody asked with surprise.

"You got it," JD said. "And this time you get to do it right. You get to be a cheerleader and all that stuff."

"That's fantastic!" Melody cried happily.

"Are you on drugs?" Cisco bellowed. "High school sucked on Earth even more than it sucks in heaven!"

"Maybe for you," Melody said, her eyes shining with happiness. "But not for me. Not for me!"

Two

"Don't look now but your sweetie pie is heading this-a-way," Cisco drawled nonchalantly, tapping Melody on the shoulder.

Melody, who had been talking with Nicole, turned around and saw Chaz threading his way through the throng of dancing teens jammed into the Heaven High gym. "Do I look okay?" she asked anxiously, pulling on the bottom of her short sweater.

"Did Marilyn Monroe look okay?" Cisco asked rhetorically.

"I saw a picture of her when she was young and she had brown hair," Nicole commented.

"Marilyn Monroe was a peroxide job?" Cisco asked. "Well, I am just totally shocked."

"My hair color is real," Melody said sincerely, touching her blonde waves. "People think I bleach it, but I don't."

"Hey, we're your roommates, we can testify that dark roots never rear their ugly little heads," Cisco said. She watched Chaz as he stopped a moment to talk to a friend. "Your boy is looking mighty fine tonight, Mel."

It was about forty-five minutes later. Melody and her friends had endured an excruciating ride to the dance with Celeste.

Celeste had prattled on and on about her grades, her wardrobe, and her nightly skin-cleansing ritual, until Nicole, Cisco, and even Melody wanted to strangle her. Finally, Cisco, who was sitting in the front seat, had retaliated by turning the car radio—which was tuned to WTHR, the Teen Heaven alternative rock radio station—louder and louder.

Celeste, though, hadn't taken the hint. She just kept raising her voice to shout over the radio. Finally Cisco had yelled "Shut up!" at the top of her lungs, and Celeste had retreated into injured silence for the rest of the ride.

Now, the three friends were standing together in a knot under the big Go BLUE ANGELS! banner that hung from the rafters. Celeste had gone to the ladies' room.

"He's so handsome," Melody breathed, watching Chaz, mesmerized by his good looks. His glossy, straight brown hair glinted in the shifting light, and he was dressed simply in a pair of black Levi's and a black T-shirt, over which he wore a black and white checked flannel shirt.

"Hi!" Chaz said to all three of the girls, as he came up to them. "Pretty crazy in here, huh?"

"Out of control," Cisco commented, glancing at the gym, which was packed with teenagers—some dancing, some just standing around and hanging out, some eating from the buffet that had been placed along one of the walls.

"It's hard to believe that so many teens have died," Nicole mused. "Although some of them have probably been here quite a while. Which means if they were on Earth, they wouldn't be teens anymore. So I don't know if technically they're still teens or not.''

"The logic of your mind is an astonishing thing," Cisco marveled.

"Thank you," Nicole said seriously.

"You look really beautiful, Melody," Chaz said shyly, smiling at her.

"You do, too," she said. "I mean, you look nice. Wonderful!"

"Want to dance?" Chaz asked Melody.

"I'd love to!" she replied.

Chaz held out his right hand, gallantly, and Melody took it. Chaz then guided her easily onto the dance floor, just as the song that was blasting over the sound system in the gym was ending.

"Time for a nice slow one," said Sunny, the housefather in their dormitory, over the gym's PA system. Sunny was acting as disc jockey for the evening.

"Time to hang on tight," Sunny growled into the mike, as he pushed a button on the console in front of him. Instantly, the classic Moody Blues song "Nights in White Satin" boomed out over the sound system.

"Give it a rest, Sunny!" some kid called out.

"Go back to the sixties!" another girl cried out.

"The Age of Aquarius is over, dude!" another kid shouted, good-naturedly.

Everyone on the gym floor cracked up. It was well known that Sunny, a handsome, barrel-chested African-American guy with an unfashionably big Afro haircut, had died in a balloon accident at the original Woodstock. He and his wife Frieda were old hippies and proud of it.

14

"Hey, just give it a listen, dudes and dudettes," Sunny suggested, his voice cutting into the song.

Some of the kids stopped dancing, but others put their arms around each other and swayed to the golden oldie.

"Want to?" Chaz asked Melody.

"Sure," Melody replied, and she stepped into Chaz's arms.

Everyone thinks Chaz and I are already hot and heavy, Melody thought, as she leaned her head against Chaz's shoulder, but actually we've never really done anything more than hold hands. Oh, he feels so wonderful . . .

"Mel, you feel fantastic," Chaz murmured into her ear.

"I was just thinking the same thing about you," Melody admitted. She closed her eyes and blissed out, moving with Chaz to the slow, sensual music, which soon came to an end.

"And now one of my faves," Sunny said through the microphone. "Here's a little Rolling Stones comin' at ya!"

The opening riff of the old Stones hit "Honky Tonk Woman" filled the air.

"We need a new DJ!" someone yelled good-naturedly.

"Hey, know how to jitterbug?" Chaz asked Melody.

"Kind of," Melody said.

"Let's go!" Chaz said. He pulled Melody into the dance. His steps got more and more complicated, until he was twirling her around and around the dance floor. Some of the kids even stopped to watch them dance. When the song finally ended, some people clapped, and Melody threw herself into Chaz's arms.

"That was so much fun!" she cried breathlessly. "Where did you learn to dance like that?"

"My mother made me take ballroom dance lessons when I was a kid," Chaz explained. "My dad thought it was wimpy and fought with her about it, but Mom won."

"I'm glad she did!" Melody said with a laugh.

"So, where did you learn to dance?" Chaz asked. He took Melody's hand and led her to the side of the gym.

"Oh, my mom made me take dancing lessons and singing lessons," Melody said. "She was convinced I was going to need them when I became a star."

Chaz leaned against the wall. "A star?"

Melody shrugged. "She was convinced I was going to have this big career . . ."

"Was that what you wanted?"

Melody looked at the floor a moment. *I haven't told Chaz very much about myself yet,* she realized. *And I don't know if I should now . . .*

She looked up at him. "It's not very interesting, really—"

"Hey, Mel, if it's about you, it's interesting to me," Chaz said.

"Well, I never wanted to be in show business at all," Melody said quietly. "I mean, I don't have any talent."

"Hey, I know you can dance!" Chaz pointed out.

Melody shrugged. "It's strange, I guess. I mean, Mom always told me I wasn't that smart, that I didn't have any talent, but I'd become this famous star anyway because—" She stopped herself. *I can't very well say because of how I look,* she realized.

"Because you're so pretty?" Chaz guessed.

Melody blushed. "I know that sounds stupid . . ."

"Well, you are beautiful, Mel," Chaz said. He shook his hair out of his eyes. "But what I don't get is why did she tell you that you weren't smart and didn't have any talent and then tell you that you were going to be a star?"

"Maybe she was just telling me the truth—about my not having any talent, anyway," Melody guessed.

"And maybe she just wanted to keep you insecure and dependent," Chaz said.

"Oh, I don't think so—"

Chaz put his arm around her shoulders. "I'm sorry. I shouldn't play amateur shrink. I don't even know very much about your mom—just that she was a waitress and she quit to manage your career."

Melody smiled. "You have a good memory."

Chaz pulled Melody close. "Your mom was wrong, Mel. You are smart. And you do have talent."

"You think so?" Melody asked, gazing up at him.

"I think so," he replied huskily.

"Okeydokey, here's the last oldie of my set," Sunny growled into the mike. "So all you angels, let me see you get up and boogie!"

The original James Brown version of the song "Shout!" filled the air. Everyone ran out on to the dance floor with a cheer. Melody and Chaz began to dance wildly with Cisco, Jake, and Nicole.

"I love this song!" Cisco yelled, bopping to the music.

"Fit!" someone yelled midway through the song, and everyone threw themselves onto the floor, writhing around to the music. Even proper Nicole joined in, laughing so hard she practically choked.

"Well, that was a first for me," Nicole said when the song ended.

Sunny then put on a slow tune by Nirvana, and Nicole slipped into Jake's arms.

"Tell me that wasn't a blast," Cisco said to no one in particular, holding the hair off her neck.

"Dance?" a guy asked, coming up behind Cisco.

She turned around. He was tall, with a blond ponytail and an earring glinting in one ear. "Do I know you?" she said.

"Nope," the guy admitted. "But I've heard about you. I'm Spencer Adams, Jake Silverman's roommate."

"Hey, in that case you're practically related," Chaz teased.

"I guess you know my roommate Nicole, who's over there dancing with your roommate," Cisco said. "And this is my other roommate, Melody, and this is Chaz."

"Hi," Spencer said, nodding at them. "So?" He held out his hand invitingly to Cisco.

"Okay," she said with a shrug. She turned back to Melody as Spencer led her on to the dance floor. "Send in the reinforcements if I'm not back in ten minutes."

"Have you ever seen him before?" Melody asked Chaz, as they watched Cisco and Spencer begin to dance.

"No," Chaz said. "He and Jake live in a different dorm." He turned to Melody. "So, how about we go outside and get some air?"

"Sounds good to me," Melody agreed.

Chaz snaked them through the crowd and then out the double doors that led to the exterior of the gym.

Outside, it was mercifully quieter. There were a few kids hanging out, cooling off. One couple was standing near a tree, passionately kissing.

"Some things are the same in heaven as they are on Earth, huh?" Chaz said with a grin.

Melody peered more closely at the kissing couple. "Why, it's Celeste!" she exclaimed. "So that's where she's been all night!"

"Who's the guy?" Chaz asked.

"I don't know, I've never seen him before," Melody said. "But whoever he is, I'm sure Nicole and Cisco would like to thank him for saving them from an evening with Celeste!"

Chaz led Melody to one of the unoccupied stone benches on the lawn of the school.

"What a night!" Chaz said. He put his arm around her.

"I love it," Melody agreed, snuggling next to Chaz.

"It was fun dancing."

"Your father really said dancing was . . . what did you call it?" Melody asked.

"Wimpy," Chaz said, looking up at the night sky. "He thought it was for girls."

"But that's silly!" Melody exclaimed.

Chaz shrugged. "Dad was a macho man—the kind of guy who crushes beer cans with his bare hands, bites the heads off chickens—"

"Come on!" Melody laughed.

"Okay, I'm exaggerating," Chaz admitted. "But he really was this strong, silent kind of guy. He loved to hunt—"

"I remember you told me you got killed in a hunting accident," Melody said softly.

"Right," Chaz said. "My father was always after me to go hunting with him. I hate hunting. I mean, what kind of sport is that—a human with a gun against a de-

fenseless animal? It makes me sick—it always did. But
. . . I didn't have the nerve to tell him. So I went hunting with him, and someone mistook me for a deer."

Melody leaned over and kissed his cheek. "I'm
sorry."

Chaz shrugged. "Well, I guess I can't be glad to
be dead, but . . . I never would have met you if it
hadn't happened!"

Melody beamed with happiness.

"The very first time I saw you," Chaz said in a
low voice, "it was like . . . like I just knew." His eyes
searched hers. "I know you probably think it's because of how you look. But—I know this sounds stupid—it felt like I was seeing into your soul or
something weird like that." He looked away from her
and gave a self-deprecating laugh. "Geez, there I go
with all that artsy-fartsy stuff, as my dad would say."

"What did he mean?" Melody asked.

"Oh, like he'd want to go to the shooting range,
and I'd want to go to an art museum. He called that
artsy-fartsy stuff."

"I've never been to an art museum," Melody admitted shyly.

"Really?" Chaz asked her.

"Well, once I did a photo shoot inside the Detroit
Institute of Arts," Melody said. "I wanted to stay and
look at the exhibits, but Mom said no."

"I wish I could take you to an art museum," Chaz
said longingly. "I always wanted to go to the Lou-
vre . . ."

"I've heard of that," Melody said. "It's an art museum in Paris, right?"

"Right," Chaz said. "I kind of paint, too—"

"You do?" Melody exclaimed.

Chaz is a painter? Melody thought. He never told

20

me that before. I think that's so amazing. And I think it's even more amazing that he hasn't even tried to kiss me yet.

Chaz shrugged. "My dad thought it was stupid." He laughed. "I guess I kind of let my dad run my life, huh?"

"I guess I kind of let my mom run *my* life," Melody said softly.

Chaz smiled at her, then he looked up at the sky. "You know," Chaz said, with wonder in his voice, "the stars up here are exactly the same as the stars Down Below."

"Amazing," Melody agreed. *And romantic,* she added to herself. *This would be a wonderful time for him to kiss me . . .*

Chaz turned to look at her. "You are so beautiful," he said softly.

Now, she thought, raising her face. *He's going to kiss me now!*

"But I want you to know, Mel, that that's not the reason I like you so much—well, it's not the *only* reason," he amended. "You're an incredible girl."

"I am?" Melody asked. *No one ever said that to me before,* she realized. *They might say I'm incredible-looking, but no one ever said I was incredible.*

"Yeah," Chaz said. "And even though I want to kiss you right now more than anything in the world, I'm not going to."

"You're not?" Melody asked, her heart sinking.

"I'm not," Chaz said. "Because if I kiss you now you'll think I'm just like all the other guys who were only after you for how you look." He stared into her eyes. "So I'll wait."

Melody gulped hard. It was everything she could do not to grab him and throw him down on the stone bench and kiss him herself. "Oh," she said in a small voice.

"But Mel," he added, gently pushing a loose strand of hair off her cheek, "I'll tell you this. When we finally do kiss, it's going to be the kiss of a lifetime."

"Well, it's Miss Hot and Bothered her own self," Cisco drawled, as Melody let herself into their suite a few hours later. "You're getting home late."

"I was with Chaz."

"We know," Nicole said from her perch on the couch. She had a bowl of popcorn propped between her legs. Cisco sat in the chair near her.

"So, was it incredible?" Cisco asked as she reached for another handful of popcorn.

"He's so wonderful," Melody said with a sigh. She sat down on her bed. Ruffy immediately jumped into her lap and she petted the kitten absentmindedly.

"Young love, true love!" Cisco sang out.

"Cisco danced over and over with Spencer," Nicole reported.

"He's nice," Cisco said. "He's a big tennis player. He said he'd teach me."

"I thought you weren't ready for a boyfriend," Nicole said.

"I'm not," Cisco insisted. She threw some popcorn in the air and caught it in her mouth. "That doesn't mean I can't have a guy friend, does it?"

"Is there any chemistry?" Nicole asked.

"Meaning what?" Cisco queried.

"Meaning, do you have friendly feelings toward him or sexual feelings toward him?" Nicole specified.

"How do I know?" Cisco snapped. "I just met the guy!"

"Chemistry is either there or not there," Nicole said distinctly. "That doesn't mean you have to act on it, of course, but—"

"Okay, okay, there's chemistry," Cisco admitted. "You happy, Madam Attorney?"

Nicole smiled smugly at Cisco, then she turned to Melody. "You're awfully quiet."

Melody threw herself back on her bed. "I think I'm in love," she said softly.

"That's wonderful!" Nicole exclaimed.

"No, it's crazy!" Melody said, sitting up again. "You're not going to believe this, but Chaz hasn't even kissed me yet! He said he's waiting so I don't think he's like every other guy who just wants to get into my pants!"

"Cool move," Cisco approved.

"But I'm dying to have him kiss me!" Melody cried. "We talked for two hours, sitting outside on the bench. And I knew I should be mature and carry on this interesting conversation with him, but all I could think about was kissing him! I must be some kind of pervert!"

"So, the shoe is on the other foot," Nicole said, nodding.

"What does that mean?" Melody asked.

"How many times have you tried to talk to a guy and all he was thinking about was kissing you?"

"So this is how it feels," Melody moaned. "Awful!"

Cisco laughed. "Well, there's a little something on your desk that ought to take your mind off of Chaz. If that doesn't work, you could try a cold shower."

"What?" Melody asked with a sigh. She got up and went over to her desk. And there was her dossier, for her very first mission Down Below.

"I can't believe I forgot all about this!" Melody exclaimed.

"Wow, you really have got it bad," Cisco said.

"JD left it?" Melody asked.

"Just a few minutes ago," Cisco reported. "He said he'd be back."

"Did you read it?" Melody asked.

"Of course not," Nicole said.

"I wanted to," Cisco admitted. "She stopped me."

"It would have been okay," Melody said, going over to her bed, picking up the dossier, and opening it. A thin sheet of paper fell to the ground. She reached down and picked it up. It was typewritten on official JD stationery.

To: Melody Monroe
From: JD
Re: Your very first mission Down Below

Congrats, babe. You're going back to high school!

Have you ever been to Nashville, Tennessee? No? How did I know the answer to that question? I'm sure Cisco could fill you in on all the background, but you're going to be leaving soon. Very soon.

Here's your mission: The girl's name is Scarlett Whitmore. And the school you're going to be attending is Whitmore High School. You got it. The school is named after the babe's family. They've been in Nashville for a really, really long time.

I gotta tell you, this girl is some piece of work. She's rich, smart, and great-looking. Basically, she's got it all, which she does not even begin to appreciate. Because she is selfish, self-centered, shallow, mean, and lazy. Oh, and did I mention a snob? Yeah, that, too.

This is what the Big Guy calls your basic waste, if you catch my drift.

Your mission? Help her change. If you don't, she'll end up squandering all the gifts the Big Guy gave her, and you know how much He frowns on that.

So, no problem, right?

You'll be in the senior class at Whitmore High School as a visiting student from your old school in Detroit. Oh, yeah, you'll be a cheerleader ("Go, Whitmore Cougars!"), which should help you out, since Miss Scarlett is a cheerleader, too. You'll be living temporarily with the Snider family. They're a really nice couple who've got a ten-year-old girl. They've got another daughter who's in college. You'll be staying in her room.

Anything else? I don't think so. You'll find everything else you need in your room. Have a blast!

"So, how does it look?" Cisco asked, as she watched Melody read the dossier.

"Well, the girl I'm supposed to help sounds awful," Melody admitted. She looked over at Cisco. "Help!"

"What's so awful about her?" Nicole asked.

JD suddenly appeared sitting on Melody's desk, casually leaning back against the wall. "How goes it?" he asked.

"You're as bad as Celeste," Cisco groused. "Don't you believe in knocking, either?"

25

JD rapped his knuckles on the desk. "So, Melody, you ready?"

"I guess so," Melody said reluctantly.

"Do I detect a certain lack of enthusiasm?" JD asked.

"I'm not complaining or anything," Melody said quickly, "but this girl Scarlett . . . she doesn't sound very . . . nice."

"She isn't," JD said. "That's the whole point."

"Right," Melody agreed. She bit her lip nervously. "But . . . she's rich and smart. Girls like that always kind of intimidated me," she admitted.

"Live, die, and learn, I always say," JD said with a shrug. He hopped off the desk and came over to Melody. "Looks like it's just about show time!"

Melody took a deep breath. "I'm ready," she said. She looked over at her roommates. "Take care of Ruffy while I'm gone. And tell Chaz—"

But she never got to finish her sentence.

Just like that, she was gone.

Three

"Well, Melody, dear, don't you look pretty," Mrs. Snider said, as Melody walked into the kitchen. "What would you like for breakfast? Kelly Anne will be here in a minute. She can make you anything you like."

Melody had arrived the night before, popping up in a car just down the block from the Sniders' house in an upscale neighborhood of Nashville called Green Hills. In her hand was an address written in JD's distinctive scrawl, followed by the line, "Everything is there waiting for you, babe. Your clothes were shipped yesterday."

As Melody drove up the Sniders' circular driveway, she had been practically overcome with fear. For one thing, the Snider were clearly rich. Their painted brick home was huge, surrounded by a vast, well-manicured lawn. The front porch alone was bigger than the entire apartment Melody had lived in with her mother, brother, and sister.

She had parked the car and then nervously walked to the Sniders' house and rung the doorbell. She had been welcomed into the Sniders' home by Mrs.

Snider, a plump, attractive, perfectly coiffed blonde-haired woman with the energy of a steamroller. Mr. Snider, a stockbroker, was just the opposite—a thin, quiet man who sat in a chair in the living room, reading books about how to better his bridge game. Both Mr. and Mrs. Snider were championship bridge players.

Although Melody felt dizzy with nerves, everything at the Sniders' had gone smoothly. They really believed she was an exchange student visiting from her high school in Detroit, Mumford High, and she'd be staying with them for a while, most likely through the end of the semester.

Melody had been shown to a beautiful room filled with high school memorabilia belonging to their daughter, Wendy, who was away at college. Mrs. Snider had informed Melody that all her belongings had arrived the day before, and Melody had found an entire wardrobe of gorgeous clothes supposedly belonging to her, but much nicer than anything she had actually owned when she really *was* in high school, already hanging in the closet and folded neatly in the dresser drawers. Mrs. Snider explained that Kelly Anne, their housekeeper, had unpacked Melody's luggage for her.

A housekeeper, Melody had thought dizzily. *They have a housekeeper. Where I come from people don't have housekeepers—they are housekeepers.*

The Sniders' ten-year-old daughter, Cindy, had timidly stuck her head into Melody's room. She was quiet and shy, wore thick glasses, and had braces on her teeth. She was clearly enthralled with Melody and could hardly speak in her presence.

Now Cindy was sitting at the breakfast table, silently chewing her cereal with bananas, staring at

Melody. Mr. Snider had his face hidden behind the morning paper.

"I'll just have toast, if that's okay," Melody said shyly, as she sat down at the breakfast table.

"Nonsense," Mrs. Snider said. "You have to eat. You need fuel to get you through the day! How about some blueberry pancakes?"

"Oh, no—"

"Eggs? Cereal?" Mrs. Snider offered.

"Whatever Cindy is eating is fine with me," Melody said.

"Well, I don't know how you girls last all morning on that little bit of food," Mrs. Snider said, pouring Melody a glass of orange juice. "There, dear," she said, setting it down in front of Melody.

"Morning," a thin young woman called cheerfully, sticking her head into the kitchen. She had pretty blue eyes and long brown hair in a braid down her back. "Oh, hey," she said, looking at Melody. "You must be Melody. I'm Kelly Anne." She had a thick, twangy southern accent Melody hadn't heard before.

"Thanks for putting my clothes away," Melody said softly.

"Oh, ain't nothing to it," Kelly Anne said cheerfully. "Say, did anyone ever tell you you look just like Marilyn Monroe?"

"Yes," Melody admitted.

"Well danged if it isn't true!" Kelly Anne exclaimed. She looked at what Melody was wearing and smiled. "I just loved that little outfit when I hung it up for you yesterday," she said.

Melody looked down at herself. After agonizing over what to wear, she had finally chosen a short, blue pleated silk skirt with a matching silk T-shirt, and a white flannel vest over it.

"Do you think it's too dressy?" Melody asked nervously.

Kelly Anne shrugged. "Danged if I know. I went to school back in Sevierville, in the mountains. We all wore jeans every day."

"Maybe I should change—"

"Oh, no," Mrs. Snider said. "You look lovely."

"But maybe kids don't dress up this much here—"

"Honey, when a girl is a pretty as you are, you are the trend starter, not the trend follower, so I wouldn't worry," Mrs. Snider said. "Besides, it's your first day."

Melody sipped her juice. "How do I get to school?" she asked shyly.

"I'll write out directions for you," Mrs. Snider offered. "It's not far. You'll love Whitmore High. Our daughter Wendy graduated from there last year. Won't she love Whitmore, honey?" Mrs. Snider asked her husband.

"Hmmm," he mumbled from behind the newspaper.

"You'll love it," Mrs. Snider said again. "And you'll make lots of friends, I'm sure. You can have them over any time you like."

"That's so nice of you—"

Mrs. Snider waved her off. "Our home is your home, Melody, dear," she said. "We've had exchange students from all over the world stay with us on and off through the years, and we've always had a wonderful experience."

I'll bet you never had one from out of this world before, Melody felt like saying, but she kept her mouth shut.

Armed with directions Melody drove herself to Whitmore High School, a sprawling red brick building that looked more like a small college campus. In the office she had received her schedule, and then she'd joined the throngs of students on their way to their first-period class. Hers was Honors American Literature.

Honors, Melody thought, gulping hard. *I was never in an honors class in my life. How will I ever keep up?*

That was only one of her worries. As she walked down the hall kids stared at her, whispered about her, but no one spoke to her. And, she realized with chagrin, she was much more dressed up than anyone else at the school.

I hate it here, she thought, sweat trickling down her spine. *I want to be beamed back up, JD! I'm scared!*

"Settle down, people, settle down," the teacher was saying when Melody walked into the classroom. It had taken her a while to find the correct room—the campus was so large—and all the other students were already in their seats. She could feel all eyes on her as she handed the teacher the pink slip she'd been given that explained that she was an exchange student, transferring in.

"Uh-huh, uh-huh," the teacher grunted, reading the pink slip. "Well, welcome," he said, looking up at Melody. He was tall and thin—almost gaunt—and he wore a silly looking red bowtie with an outdated suit. "I'm Dr. Capelli. This is Honors American Lit. Allegedly the people in this room are smart, and I'm sure that applies to you, too."

Melody attempted a smile.

"Class, this is Melody Monroe," Dr. Capelli read off the pink slip. A few kids snickered.

"What is it, really?" a girl in the front row asked.

"That's really it," Melody said.

"Works for me," a cute guy in the back called out, grinning at Melody.

"You can take a seat next to Mr. Bowman, the young man grinning at you from the back of the room," Dr. Capelli said.

For the next hour Melody listened as the class discussed the novel they had all just finished reading, *The Grapes of Wrath*, by John Steinbeck. Since she hadn't read the book, she was totally lost. Just when her mind was wandering, she heard Dr. Capelli say, "Scarlett? What do you think?"

Scarlett. Unless there were two Scarletts, it had to be her. Melody looked across the room at the girl Mr. Capelli was staring at.

"What was the question?" Scarlett asked in a lazy voice.

"If you had been listening, you would know what the question was, Miss Whitmore," Dr. Capelli said.

That's her, Melody realized. *My assignment.* She studied the girl carefully. Scarlett had long, straight honey-blonde hair with lighter blonde streaks around her hairline. Her face was a perfect oval, with high cheekbones, a thin nose, and full lips. Her eyes were light—Melody couldn't tell exactly what color from across the room—and although she wore subtle makeup, her beauty was natural and fresh. She wore a blue-and-white Whitmore High cheerleading outfit.

"I guess that means I wasn't listening then," Scarlett admitted casually, tossing her hair off her face. Next to her a black-haired girl, also wearing a cheerleading outfit, snickered at Scarlett's reply.

"I asked how the class struggles in *Grapes of*

Wrath could be compared with class struggle today," Dr. Capelli repeated in an even tone.

Scarlett shrugged.

"Meaning you have no idea?" Dr. Capelli asked, "or meaning you are too lazy to entertain an idea?"

Scarlett sighed. "The way I see it is this. No one in America has to be poor. If people are poor, it's just because they're lazy or something."

"Oh, really," Dr. Capelli said. "And how do you earn your money, Miss Whitmore, if I might be so bold as to ask?"

At that moment the bell rang, which meant that Melody never got to hear Scarlett's answer. As Melody headed for the door, she found Scarlett and the black-haired cheerleader waiting there for her.

"Hi," Scarlett said coolly, looking Melody over. "I'm Scarlett Whitmore. This is Jennifer Powter."

"I'm—"

"We know who you are," Jennifer said. "Our cheerleading coach, Miss Sunder, told us you were going to be on the squad."

"Or as we call her Miss Thunder," Scarlett said, "as in thighs. We are talking thunder thighs for days."

Jennifer laughed. "No kidding! Anyway, she said you were head cheerleader at your high school in Detroit and that you're really, really good."

"I am?" Melody asked with dismay. "I mean, I am!" she added quickly.

"So, we have practice after school today," Scarlett continued. "It's a total bore, but we have to go."

"I'll be there," Melody promised.

"We can probably all fake having our periods and get out early," Scarlett suggested. "Then Thunder

Thighs can do her stuff with the real rah-rah types and we can escape.''

"Sounds good to me," Melody said. From behind her she heard a group of kids making loud snorting noises, and she turned around.

"Oink, oink!" a short boy cried, staring at a girl who was hurrying past.

"Soowee!" another boy catcalled gleefully, then the two boys fell over each other laughing.

Melody looked at the girl they were making fun of. She was very fat, with bright-red frizzy hair that stuck straight out from her head. As the boys laughed at her she stared ahead, pretending not to hear, but her face turned bright red.

"Hey, Porky!" the first boy called. "How many porkchops did you eat for breakfast?"

The girl hurried on, not answering.

"That's Corky McGee," Jennifer explained.

"Those boys shouldn't tease her like that," Melody said angrily.

"Please!" Scarlett scoffed. "Porky-Corky is disgusting! I can't even stand to look at all that lard!"

"She's an insult to this school, that's what she is," Jennifer agreed.

"But it's horrible to laugh at her that way!" Melody insisted.

"Hey, maybe it'll get her to go on a diet," Scarlett said with a shrug.

"So, what's your next class?" Jennifer asked.

Melody peered at her pink slip. "Art History," she said.

"We're in Chemistry," Scarlett said, rolling her eyes. "So, we'll see you later."

"Okay," Melody said. "It was nice to meet you."

Scarlett scrutinized Melody for a moment. "Listen, are you for real?"

"What do you mean?" Melody asked, her heart pounding in her chest.

"I mean, the whole Marilyn Monroe thing, the voice, the look—"

"It's just the way I am," Melody said.

Scarlett thought for a moment. "Okay, it's cool," she decided. "Just one word of advice, though."

"Sure," Melody said.

"See that guy?" She pointed down the hall toward a handsome black-haired guy, medium height, who was talking with a whole group of kids.

"Uh-huh," Melody said. "Who is he?"

"Jeff Walker." Scarlett smiled nastily. "And he's mine. You touch him, you die. See ya."

Then she and Jennifer strode away.

Melody stared at her reflection in the floor-length mirror in the girls' locker room. She had just put on the Whitmore High cheerleading outfit Miss Sunder had given her.

I really do look like a cheerleader, Melody realized, turning this way and that in the mirror. *I envied the cheerleaders at my high school so much. And now I am one. Except for the minor detail that I've never done so much as a cartwheel in my entire life.*

"I hope you're planning to help me get through this, JD," she said, staring up at the ceiling.

"Who are you talking to?" Jennifer asked, coming into the locker room.

"Oh, no one," Melody said quickly.

"Well, come on out. Thunder Thighs wants to see you strut your stuff," Jennifer said.

Melody followed Jennifer out into the gym, where the eight Whitmore High cheerleaders were waiting. Melody felt as if she was facing a firing squad.

"So, Melody," Miss Sunder said, grinning broadly, "I noticed on your records that you're a gymnastics champion and that your cheerleading squad won the state finals the last two years in a row!"

"Uh . . . right!" Melody said. Sweat broke out on her upper lip.

"Well, some of the girls on this squad are quite talented," Miss Sunder said, "but unfortunately discipline has been a problem." She gave Scarlett a sharp look. Scarlett yawned.

"We're hoping you can pep us up some!" Miss Sunder said. "Maybe you could show us one of your favorite routines—one of the more gymnastic ones would be great!"

Please, please, please, JD, Melody thought in a panic, *don't let me make a total fool out of myself.*

And then, in a flash, Melody knew that she could do it. All of a sudden it was as if she had been doing cheerleading and gymnastics for years. She could *feel* it in her mind.

"We do this one to the old rock song 'Shout,' " Melody explained, since it was the first thing that came into her head. "It's part of our half-time show." And then she proceeded to dance, twirl, and strut. She did double cartwheels, back flips, and one-handed legovers. And she finished with a series of flips across the gym, a triple pirouette, and she landed in the splits.

"Incredible!" Miss Sunder yelled, applauding wildly. "Wasn't that incredible, ya'll?"

"You're really good," Scarlett acknowledged, giving her hair its usual flip.

"I could show you guys the whole routine, if you like," Melody offered.

"How about if we make up our own but incorporate some of those moves!" suggested a petite brunette named Missy. "I'd love to learn!"

"Me, too!" a girl named Lyndi agreed. "We might even have a shot at the state finals if we could do that!"

Scarlett rolled her eyes at Jennifer and another beautiful girl named Beth. Jennifer and Beth nodded in agreement.

"I think that's a fantastic idea," Miss Sunder said. "It'll take a lot of work, girls, but it'll be worth it!"

"Oh, Miss Sunder!" Scarlett called out, her hands over her stomach. "I'm having really bad cramps."

"Me, too," Jennifer said.

"Wow, what a coincidence!" Beth exclaimed. "I have terrible cramps, too!"

"Girls . . ." Miss Sunder said dubiously.

"Well, you know how it is, Miss Sunder," Scarlett said innocently. "When girls are together all the time, they end up on the same cycle. I guess that's just what happened!"

"We're gonna have to go lie down," Jennifer said.

"Right away," Beth added.

Miss Sunder sighed. "Sometimes I wonder if you girls take cheerleading seriously."

"Oh, we do," Scarlett assured her, her voice dripping sincerity. "Cheerleading is our life. Well, 'bye now. Have a good practice." She, Jennifer, and Beth headed for the locker room, giggling with each other.

"All right, girls," Miss Sunder said loudly. "We'll continue without them. Let's show Melody some of our cheers, shall we?"

Melody watched Scarlett as she disappeared into the locker room with her friends. JD was right, she thought to herself with distaste. She is one of the most obnoxious, cruelest, most self-centered, laziest girls I've ever met in my life.

And I'm her angel.

Four

"Excuse me," a girl with strawberry-blonde hair, who looked like a sophomore, said to Melody. "Is anyone sitting here?" She pointed to the empty seat at Melody's table.

Melody looked up from the American art history book she'd been buried in for the last half hour, while her thoughts had been ricocheting back and forth from the paintings in the book to the real reason she was here Down Below—Scarlett Whitmore.

What am I going to do about her? Melody had pondered, over and over again. She is just so . . . so mean. Frankly, it's intimidating! I feel like she could turn on anyone at any minute. I'm lucky that she's nice to me, but that's probably only because she thinks I'm pretty. But if she knew how poor I really was back in Detroit, she'd never give me the time of day.

"So, is it okay?" the girl asked again. "Because there's no other table to sit at."

"Oh, sure," Melody said. "Sorry, I was thinking about something else."

It was now an hour after cheerleading practice. In the locker room afterward, Melody had heard a bunch

39

of girls chatting about Bongo Java, a new coffeehouse that had opened on Belmont Boulevard across from Belmont University.

Since she didn't have to be home at the Sniders's for dinner until seven-thirty, she decided she'd drive over and check it out.

Now, this is something I'd never have done when I was alive, Melody had thought, as she drove herself over to the new club in her Mustang. *I'd definitely have been too afraid to go in alone!*

But Melody had done it, and now here she was, sitting by herself, drinking coffee and actually—to her shock—*studying*, when the redhead had approached her.

The girl peered at Melody's art book. "What's *that*?" She pointed at a painting called *Nighthawks* by Edward Hopper. It featured a few lonely looking people in a late-night diner.

"It's eerie, isn't it?" Melody said. "I'm studying this artist for a class at school."

"Kinda spooky," the girl agreed. She sat opposite Melody. "It's really packed in here, huh? So is it okay if my friends come and sit here, too?" she asked. "You don't mind?"

"It's okay with me," Melody said shyly. "There's plenty of room."

"Cool!" the girl said. Then she waved to two other girls who were standing up at the front counter, ordering their own coffee. The girls bustled over.

"We're soooo lucky—this girl will share her table," the first girl said to her friends. "These are like the last three seats in this entire place."

"Everyone hangs out here," agreed her friend, taking a sip of hot chocolate from her cup as she sat down. She was pretty and plump, with short, shaggy brown hair. "So, what's your name?"

"Melody," Melody said, closing her art history book after carefully marking its place. "Melody Monroe."

"You're so gorgeous, I hate you!" the third girl blurted out, staring at Melody. The third girl had long, gorgeous wavy dark hair that fell halfway down her back.

"Sarah!" the first girl scolded her.

"Sorry," Sarah said sheepishly. "I just wish I looked like you. So ignore me, because I'm totally jealous."

"Sometimes I wish I had hair like yours," Melody said softly.

"Really?" Sarah asked, shocked. "Because your own hair is so gorgeous!"

"Well, yours is even nicer," Melody said kindly, taking a sip of her drink. "I always wanted long, dark hair."

"Wow," Sarah said. "Anyway, you'd look great even if your head was shaved."

"Thanks, Sarah," Melody said.

"My name's Sara, too," said the girl with strawberry-blonde hair. "No *H*."

"Me, too," chimed in the third girl, who was thinner and shorter than the others. "I'm Sayrah, with an *H*. And a *Y*."

"Sarah, Sara, and Sayrah," the three said together, as if they'd done it a million times. Then they all cracked up.

"You're all named Sarah?" Melody asked them. "I can't believe it!"

"Yup," Sayrah said, taking a sip of her own fra-

41

grant coffee. "It drives our teachers crazy that we're all friends, too."

"We've been buds like, forever," Sarah said.

"Do you go to Whitmore?" Melody asked. "Because I just started there."

"Harpeth Hall," Sara said. "We all three go there."

"It's great," Sayrah chimed in. "We've got a great drama program." She bit into a piece of carrot cake she'd also purchased at the front counter. "I am so totally starved."

"Your mother will kill you if she sees you eating cake," Sara said, looking toward the front door.

"Relax," Sayrah said, cutting off another piece of the cake. "The moms aren't due to pick us up for another half hour."

"I can't wait 'til I get my driver's license!" Sara exclaimed.

"So, what's Harpeth Hall like?" Melody asked.

"All girls," Sarah explained. "No guys at all. Which I think really stinks!"

"I kind of like it," Sara said.

"Well, everyone knows you're kind of crazy," Sayrah teased. "Mmmm, this cake is to die for."

Melody smiled at them. They remind me of a younger version of me, Nicole, and Cisco, she thought. I miss them so much already.

"The best thing about Harpeth Hall is the drama program," Sayrah repeated, scooping up with a fork the last of her cake. "I want to grow up to be a famous actress."

"Me too," Sara said.

"Me three," Sarah chimed in. "We're gonna share an apartment in New York!"

"What about you?" Sayrah asked Melody.

42

I guess I'll never know, Melody thought. I wonder if you do get older in Teen Heaven.

"I'm not sure," Melody answered. Then she looked down at her art book.

"I'm getting interested in art," she added quickly, thinking about Chaz Denton and how important art was to him.

"You're so gorgeous," Sara said, "I figured for sure you want to be a movie star."

"Not me," Melody said quickly. "For one thing, I don't have any talent."

"So?" Sarah said. "Neither do half the girls in Hollywood. Look at all the models who become actresses!"

"I don't think I could ever act," Melody said.

"You don't think it would be fun to be rich and famous and have every guy in the whole world drooling over you?" Sayrah asked.

"Sayrah, she's probably already got every guy drooling over her," Sarah said.

"Yeah, that's true," Sayrah agreed. She looked over at Melody. "Hey, if you're interested in art, you should check out the exhibit that's coming to town!"

Melody told her she didn't know anything about it, so Sayrah told her all about the traveling exhibit from the Whitney Museum in New York that was coming to the Tennessee State Museum in a week or so.

"That sounds fantastic!" Melody exclaimed. "I'll definitely check it out!" It'll be my very first trip to an art museum, she thought proudly. I wish I could tell Chaz.

A car horn beeped three times outside. And then another horn beeped. And then another.

"It's the *moms*," Sara said with a sigh, slurping down the last of her hot chocolate.

"They all three come together," Sarah explained.

"Then they beep in unison," Sayrah added. "How lame is that?"

"Anyway, we're outta here," Sarah said. "See you again sometime." She paused, then asked, "Hey, are you trying out for *Bus Stop*?" as she got up from the table. "Whitmore's putting it on, right? We have tons of friends at your school who are trying out."

"Right," Melody said. She'd seen a notice about auditions up on the bulletin board at school.

"Go for it!" Sarah urged. "We'll come see you in it."

"Right," Sayrah chimed in. "We see all the school plays."

"Oh, I'm sure I wouldn't get a part," Melody said.

"I bet Scarlett Whitmore's trying out," Sarah mused out loud. "She's such a bi—"

Sara lightly clamped her hand over Sarah's mouth. "Rhymes with witch," she filled in for her friend. "We made a pact to clean up our language, remember?"

"Yeah, but Scarlett Whitmore deserves an exception to the pact," Sarah said, making a face. "Well, we're outta here. Nice meeting you!"

I won't argue with you about Scarlett Whitmore, Melody thought, as she watched the three nice girls from Harpeth Hall school leave. She's definitely a rhymes-with-witch. And what's worse, she's *my* rhymes-with-witch.

"Corky McGee!" called out the studious-looking guy running the auditions, as he looked down at the sign-up sheet he had attached to his clipboard.

"Oink, oink," squealed a couple of guys who were

sitting next to Melody in the school auditorium. Corky, who was walking up the center aisle, heard them. Her fair skin burned bright red.

"Here, girl!" one of the boys yelled. "Slops time!"

"Oink, oink," the other guy snorted. He looked over at Melody and gave her a knowing wink.

Melody stared back at the guy coldly. What jerks. They are so mean to her, Melody thought. What did Corky ever do to them? Why doesn't the teacher say anything?

It was now the next day after school, and, as the three girls from Harpeth Hall had mentioned, auditions for *Bus Stop* were taking place. Scarlett had told Melody earlier in the day that she was going to try out.

"It's this play about this gorgeous girl from Hollywood who's a singer, and she's on this bus," Scarlett had told her, "and this cute cowboy is in love with her and he's following her across the country. And there's a snowstorm and the bus has to stop in this rural cafe. Cherie gets to wear really cute outfits."

"Sounds interesting," Melody had said politely.

"I'm going to get the lead," Scarlett had told her, with her usual hair flip. Her two sidekicks, Jennifer and Beth, immediately agreed that of course Scarlett would get the lead.

Melody had made a very quick decision. Normally, she'd be scared to death of being in a play. But she told herself that she should try out for *Bus Stop* too, because if Scarlett was cast, it would be a great chance for her to be around Scarlett more so that she could try and influence her to change her life.

Not that anybody seems to be an influence on Scarlett Whitmore, Melody sighed to herself, ignoring the mean guys as she watched Corky climb the three steps up to the stage.

"Corky McGee!" the stage manager called out again.

"You mean Porky!" shouted one of the guys next to Melody, and many of the kids in the room cracked up.

"Quiet, please," said the drama teacher, Ms. Russell. She was a tall, thin woman with a long nose and very thin, birdlike legs.

"For whom are you auditioning?" Ms. Russell asked.

"For Cherie," Corky said, her voice shaking with nerves.

Scarlett, who was sitting next to Melody, cracked up. "I am just so sure," she drawled. "Cherie is supposed to be beautiful. So just give me a major break."

Melody looked up at Corky, who stood bravely by herself in the center of the stage while kids all around laughed at her. Corky tugged self-consciously at the oversized black sweater she wore, trying in vain to pull it away from the rolls of fat that circled her abdomen.

"You're auditioning for Cherie?" Ms. Russell asked coldly.

"Yes, ma'am," Corky repeated, twirling her frizzy red hair nervously.

"Very well," Ms. Russell said. "What monologue are you going to do for us?"

"This is the role of Flora from *Twenty-seven Wagons Full of Cotton* by Tennessee Williams," Corky said.

Then Corky began her monologue. Melody watched her, her jaw agape.

Corky was brilliant. Better than brilliant.

Although some kids talked all the way through Corky's monologue, others listened, and some even applauded when Corky finished. Melody applauded, too.

"Are you out of your mind?" Scarlett asked Melody. "What are you doing applauding for that fat pig?"

"She was wonderful," Melody said.

"You'll only encourage her if you applaud," Beth said snottily. "Scarlett's right."

"Thank you, Corky," Ms. Russell said, her voice still cold. "That was very good. Let's take a ten-minute break, everyone."

Corky came off the stage as everyone stood up and stretched their legs, chatting and talking excitedly. She took a seat by herself, over by the side of the theater. No one came over to talk to her.

Impetuously Melody got up and went over to Corky. "That was really good," Melody told her.

"Gee, thanks," Corky said, her voice very wary.

"I'm Melody," Melody said. "Melody Monroe."

"Corky," the girl mumbled, pushing some frizzy hair behind her ear.

"I mean it," Melody continued, sitting down next to Corky. "You are really, really talented."

"Thanks," Corky said quietly.

At that moment Scarlett, Beth, and Jennifer walked up the aisle past them. "Hey, Mel," Scarlett called out, "what are you doing? I thought you didn't eat *pig*!"

Scarlett and her friends cackled and walked away. Melody turned to Corky, who had turned as crimson as her red hair.

"She's not very nice," Melody said.

"Duh," Corky replied.

"I don't know why she's so mean to you," Melody said.

Corky looked at Melody coldly. "She seems to be your friend," she observed.

"She's not my friend," Melody defended herself.

"Look," Corky said, her eyes narrowing. "I'm not stupid. Scarlett Whitmore never talks to anyone unless she's their friend."

"But—"

Corky stood up. "So why don't you just leave me alone?"

"But—"

It was too late. Corky McGee had turned and walked away.

"May I have your attention!" the voice boomed out into Melody's World History class. "May I have your attention, please."

Everyone in the class—the last one of the day—looked up at the loudspeaker on the wall and at the same time started to put their books away. Announcements were made at the end of the school day, so the loudspeaker voice was a signal for kids to start to pack it in.

"Attention all students," the vice-principal's voice boomed out. "Don't forget the canned goods drive which began last week. The wrestling team has an away match today at Brentwood High School. Come show your support. And the cast and crew list for our production of *Bus Stop* is now posted outside the auditorium. That is all."

Just at that moment the bell rang, and the school day was over.

"Let's go see—" Melody began, trying to be friendly, as she turned to Corky, who sat a couple of seats away from her in class. But Corky, who'd ignored her since their time in the audition the day before, had already left.

Okay, I'll have to go by myself. I doubt I got cast for anything, though, Melody thought. I don't think I have very much talent, and I don't think I gave a very good audition. But Corky's probably in.

Melody turned left out of the classroom and walked a few steps down the corridor toward the auditorium. There, posted outside the auditorium, was the cast list. Melody held her breath and took a quick look at it.

"Oh, gosh!" Melody breathed out loud. She felt ridiculously happy. She had actually been given a part—a good part—the second female lead, in fact. She had been cast as the young, romantic waitress in the café.

Melody quickly scanned the list to see who had been given the role of Cherie, certain that it would be Corky.

It wasn't. It was Scarlett.

Corky's name was listed as stage manager.

But that's not fair, Melody thought to herself. Corky was wonderful, and Scarlett was awful. I saw both of them audition, and there was no comparison.

"Hey, Melody," a guy called to her. "Congrats!"

Melody turned around. It was Jeff Walker, Scarlett's boyfriend. With him was Gray Morse, Jeff's friend, a really cute guy who Melody knew had his own band. Melody thought Gray looked kind of like Brad Pitt, but younger.

"Thanks," Melody told Jeff. "I really didn't think I'd get it."

"C'mon, we saw your audition," Gray said.

"You did?" Melody replied, working her way out

of the knot of people gathered around the posted list.

"Sure," Jeff said easily. "Yours and Scarlett's."

"Well," Melody said hesitantly, "I'm glad we're both in the play."

Jeff laughed. "If Scarlett hadn't gotten in she probably would have set the school on fire or something."

"She's got quite a temper," Gray agreed. He turned to Melody. "So, we were thinking maybe the four of us could, like, go hang out and celebrate."

He's asking me out, Melody realized. What am I supposed to do? I'm in love with Chaz, and I'd feel like I was cheating on him! On the other hand, we'd be going out with Scarlett and Jeff, and I need to spend as much time around Scarlett as I possibly can, whether I want to or not.

"That sounds like fun," Melody agreed. "But . . . I have a boyfriend."

Gray raised his eyebrows. "Really," he said. "Who?"

"His name is Chaz," Melody said. "Back home."

"You're from Detroit, right?" Gray asked.

"Right."

"But you're here now," Jeff pointed out.

"Yeah," Melody said softly, "but I'll be going home eventually . . ."

"So you're not going to have any fun for the whole time that you're in Nashville?" Jeff asked.

"I wouldn't want my boyfriend back home dating anyone else while I'm gone," Melody explained. "So . . ."

"Well," Gray said, "when you get tired of your long-distance romance, remember I asked you out first. Catch you later."

As Gray and Jeff departed, and the crowd had nearly completely thinned out, Melody watched as

50

Corky McGee edged over and took a quick look at the posted list. Corky's face fell when she saw that she didn't get a part.

"I'm sorry," Melody said, going over to her. "You deserved to get the lead."

"Yeah," Corky said, "sure I deserved it. But did I get it? I did not." Tears came to Corky's eyes, which she quickly brushed away with the back of her hand.

"I just don't understand it," Melody said with frustration. "Scarlett wasn't nearly as good as you were."

"Listen," Corky said in a cold voice, "you're new here. Scarlett Whitmore always gets the leads. Even if she can't act her way out of a paper bag."

"But—"

"Scarlett is gorgeous," Corky sneered. "And she has the entire school and half of the faculty wrapped around her rich and powerful little finger. Plus Ms. Russell wouldn't know talent if it reached up and bit her in the butt!"

"But—"

"But nothing," Corky said. "It never changes. Scarlett this, and Scarlett that. And everyone oinks at fat me. That is just the way it is."

"But—"

It was no use. For the second time in less than twenty-four hours, Corky McGee huffily turned on her heels and left Melody staring at her departing back.

Five

"I don't know what you're so flipped out about," Scarlett said to Melody as they walked into the Green Hills Mall. "Gray is really cool and really popular."

It was the next day. Scarlett and Beth had planned a shopping trip to the mall after school, but in English class Beth told Scarlett she had to go home and do something for her mom. So Scarlett had invited Melody to come instead.

She'd also talked Melody into going out that evening with her, Jeff, and Gray. They were going out to dinner at a place called Barry C's. Scarlett's parents were friends with the owners.

"Gray seems really nice," Melody said as they walked into the mall. "But I feel like I'm being disloyal to Chaz . . ."

"Oh, please," Scarlett scoffed. "He doesn't expect you to live like a nun while you're here, does he?"

"No—"

"We'll have a blast," Scarlett said. "Now, let's pick out some incredible new clothes for tonight."

Melody thought about the credit card, made out in her name, that was in her purse. She had found it with all the other things that were supposedly "hers" at the Sniders's house. I wonder what my credit limit is, she mused. Then she smiled. Well, whatever it is, it's a whole lot higher than it was when I was alive!

"Oh, God, look at that outfit," Scarlett said, pointing to the outfit displayed in the window of an expensive boutique. It featured a lime-green pants suit with gold nautical detailing. "How hideous is that?"

"It's ugly," Melody agreed.

"The buyer in that store has no taste," Scarlett decreed. "No one cool ever shops in there. Come on, we'll go down to Felicia's."

They walked around the corner and entered a boutique with the name FELICIA in tiny gold script on the window. An impeccably groomed, slender young woman in black crepe pants, a black body suit, and a fitted black silk jacket, walked over to the girls. "Scarlett!" she exclaimed happily. "How nice to see you."

"Hi," Scarlett said diffidently. "This is my friend, Melody. This is Felicia's daughter, Ashton," she added to Melody.

"Hi," Melody said.

Scarlett turned back to Ashton. "We're looking for outfits for tonight," she said. "We're celebrating. I got the lead in the school play."

And I got the second lead, Melody added in her mind. But I guess Scarlett doesn't even think about that.

"That's wonderful," Ashton said. "What kind of things were you interested in?"

"Oh, we'll just browse," Scarlett said.

"There are some lovely new designer outfits back along the wall," Ashton suggested.

Scarlett walked back to the rack of designer clothes and began to sort through them. She pulled out a white silk minidress with a gold collar and cuffs. "You like this?" she asked Melody.

"It's beautiful," Melody said honestly. She peeked at the price tag—eight hundred and forty dollars.

"It's okay," Scarlett said. "Hold on to it for me." She handed the dress to Melody. She moved a few more dresses around, then pulled out a fitted jersey dress with a high neckline that dipped in the back to below the waist. "Sexy, huh?" Scarlett said.

"Very," Melody agreed. She caught a look at the price tag—nine hundred dollars. "It's so expensive," she added.

"It would look hot on you," Scarlett said. "You should get it. You can afford it, can't you?"

"I don't know . . ." Melody hesitated. "It just seems like so much money to spend on one dress."

"So?" Scarlett asked. She held up a black dress, decided against it, then put it back.

"So, I can't help but think about—I don't know— all the people who don't have enough money for even inexpensive clothes," Melody said softly.

"What does that have to do with us?" Scarlett asked.

"Well, people are connected to each other," Melody tried to explain.

"Look, if I buy a cheap dress, some bum is not going to have any more money, is he?" Scarlett asked. She pulled out a two-piece black chiffon outfit and handed it to Melody to hold.

"What if . . . what if we bought less expensive dresses, and then gave the money we saved to . . . a charity," Melody suggested.

Scarlett stared at her. "You've got to be kidding."

"No, I'm not," Melody said.

Scarlett laughed. "Look, my parents give a lot of money to charity, okay? My mom works on all these charity committees. Personally, I think it's a total waste of time. She only does it because my father totally ignores her. Actually, I think he's sleeping with his secretary."

Melody was shocked. "Really?" she asked. "That's terrible! Your mother must be so upset!"

Scarlett shrugged. "She's not about to open her mouth. She enjoys spending Dad's money too much. Let's go try these on."

After trying on many different outfits, Scarlett bought the white dress, the black outfit, and two cashmere sweaters. Melody tried on a lot of things but just couldn't bring herself to spend that kind of money—more than the rent her mother paid on their apartment in Detroit.

"Let's go get some food," Scarlett said. "I'm starved."

They went to the food court and bought slices of pizza and drinks, then they sat down to eat.

"So, how do you like Nashville so far?" Scarlett asked, taking a sip of her Coke.

"It's really nice," Melody said.

"It's a bore," Scarlett pronounced. "I am going as far away for college as I can get. Maybe the University of Miami. It's supposed to be a real party school. I am definitely not going to college to *study*!"

Melody took a bite of her pizza, at a loss for words. I don't even know how to make conversation with her, she thought miserably. My stupid attempt to get her to give money to charity was ridiculous. I have to come up with something better than that.

Melody tried a new tact. "Corky McGee is really

talented, don't you think?'' she said thoughtfully.

Scarlett practically choked on her pizza. ''What brought that up?''

''I don't know,'' Melody said. ''I was just thinking about what a great audition she gave for the play.''

''If I looked like her, I'd kill myself,'' Scarlett said, taking another bite of pizza.

''Well, what if you weren't born as lucky as you are?'' Melody asked softly. ''What if you were born with . . . with a weight problem? Or with bad hair?''

''If I had a weight problem, I'd go on a diet,'' Scarlett said. ''And if I had bad hair, I'd go to a good hairdresser, okay?''

''But it isn't that easy for everyone—''

''Honestly, Melody, what is it with you?'' Scarlett asked. ''Let me just give you a few words of advice. If you go around hanging out with a girl like Porky, you aren't going to be very popular for very long, no matter how cute you are.''

''But don't you think it's superficial to judge people only by how they look?'' Melody asked.

Scarlett looked at her blankly. ''Ask me if I care.''

Melody sighed. This is getting me exactly nowhere. I have no idea how to get through to her!

''Have you ever been scared, Scarlett?'' she asked.

''What are you talking about?''

''I mean, have you ever felt . . . I don't know . . . insecure?''

''No,'' Scarlett said bluntly.

''Never?''

Scarlett thought a minute. ''Well, once. They were picking homecoming court last year, and this group of losers started a campaign against me. So I thought maybe I wouldn't win. It would have been totally mortifying. I had to win.''

"So you did win, then?" Melody asked.

"Yeah," Scarlett said with a smile. "You want to get some ice cream?"

"Did you ever think that maybe you want more out of life than . . . just having fun?" Melody pressed.

"No," Scarlett said. "And you are really starting to annoy me." She got up and walked over to the ice cream booth. Melody finally got up and went after her.

"I didn't mean to annoy you," Melody said.

"What is it with you?" Scarlett asked again. She scanned the ice cream flavors. "I'm having a double-dip," she announced.

"It's lucky you don't gain weight, isn't it." Melody said. "I have to watch every bite I put in my mouth."

"Not me," Scarlett said. She turned to the girl behind the ice cream counter and ordered her cone.

"Hey, Scarlett!" a cute brunette called, hurrying over to them.

"Oh, hi, Cheryl," Scarlett said, licking her ice cream cone. "Do you guys know each other?" They didn't. Scarlett quickly introduced them. "Cheryl went to Whitmore last year, but now she goes to Brentwood."

"I got kicked out for smoking a joint in the girls' john," Cheryl said, rolling her eyes.

"I know two guys who skin-pop heroin at school," Scarlett said. "And you got kicked out for one stupid joint."

"Tell me about it," Cheryl agreed. "So, listen," Cheryl said, "my mother was at the school board meeting last night. You are not going to believe what they voted in. All seniors at public high schools in

Nashville have to do community service to graduate, starting with our class."

"What, like pick up trash or something?" Scarlett asked, horrified.

"There's going to be a whole list of stuff we can choose from," Cheryl reported. "My parents spoke against it. They said we're busy enough with school and clubs and homework, and it's totally unfair to force us to do this stuff, but they lost."

"God, it kills me that I can't go to private school," Scarlett fumed.

"Hey, did you hear that Liza Murray was caught sniffing glue with Todd Parkinson?"

"Get out of here!" Scarlett exclaimed.

"That's what I heard," Cheryl said. "They were behind the school and the vice principal caught them. Oh, and I heard that Gray is going crazy over some new babe who is this total fox, and his old girlfriend Tristan is, like, ready to slit her wrists."

Scarlett laughed and Melody blushed. "You're looking at the new babe," she said.

"It's you?" Cheryl asked. "Wow, you're so lucky! Gray is so fine!"

"I have a boyfriend—"

"Send Gray over to me, then," Cheryl said. "I'd get down and dirty with him in a New York minute!" She turned back to Scarlett. "Oh, God, listen to this. My mother found my birth control pills."

"Did she kill you?" Scarlett asked.

"She cried and then she went to church and prayed for my soul and now she isn't speaking to me," Cheryl reported. "On the other hand, she didn't take the pills away, so I'm okay." She looked at her watch. "Wow, I gotta motor. I am, like, totally late. Tell everyone at Whitmore I said hi! I really miss you guys!"

"We really miss you, too!" Scarlett exclaimed.

" 'Bye!" Cheryl dashed off through the mall.

"Were you good friends when she went to Whitmore?" Melody asked politely.

"Are you kidding?" Scarlett said. "Cheryl is a slut."

"That's a terrible thing to say!" Melody protested.

"It's the truth," Scarlett said. "She did it with, like, every guy on the football team. She got drunk at some party and blacked out and every guy did it with her. Everyone knows about it."

Melody was shocked. "But that doesn't make her a slut! She was passed out! That's rape!"

"Hey, no one forced her," Scarlett said.

"But she had passed out," Melody insisted.

"Look, it's not my problem," Scarlett said. "I'm very particular about who I sleep with. Jeff is only the second. How many guys have you done it with?"

Melody blushed with embarrassment.

Scarlett laughed. "I can't believe you're blushing! Why, did you do it with the whole football team, too?"

"No!" Melody said quickly. It made her really angry when people assumed that she was fast just because of how she looked. The truth of the matter was that Melody was a virgin. "Actually, I haven't done it with anyone."

"Come on . . ." Scarlett said dubiously.

"It's true."

"Not even what's-his-name?" Scarlett asked incredulously.

"Chaz," Melody filled in. *Actually I haven't even kissed him yet*, she added to herself.

"So you really *do* live like a nun," Scarlett said,

finishing her ice cream cone. "Well, I'll tell you this. If you want to get Gray, you're going to have to put out."

"But I don't want to get Gray," Melody reminded Scarlett.

Scarlett laughed. "That will make him want you even more. A guy like Gray always wants what he can't have. This ought to be amusing!"

Melody sighed. I am getting nowhere with her fast, she thought to herself. And I don't see myself making any progress anytime soon.

Melody looked at the clock on her nightstand. She only had an hour before her double date. She'd just gotten out of a long bubble bath, and she lay on her bed at the Sniders's house wrapped in a beautiful black velvet robe with a white silk collar. She sighed deeply, lost in thought.

Let's face it, I'm getting nowhere with Scarlett. How can I help her when I don't even like her?

"I must be the world's worst Teen Angel ever," Melody said out loud in her breathy voice.

"Not even in the ballpark, babe," said JD, who had popped up on top of the TV, sitting with his legs crossed, Buddha-fashion.

"JD!" Melody exclaimed. She quickly made sure her robe was closed. "I'm so glad to see you!"

"So, how's life in the fast lane?" JD asked.

"Cheerleading is fun," Melody said. ."And some of the kids at Whitmore High are really nice. Oh! And I'm in the school play! I hope that's okay. I mean, what if I'm not still here when the play goes on?"

"Not to worry," JD said.

"At the rate I'm going I'll be here forever," Melody said. "I'm having a little trouble with Scarlett . . ."

"Yeah, I know," JD said. "I told you, she's some piece of work."

"Why is she awful to everyone?" Melody asked.

"That's one of the things you need to figure out," JD pointed out.

"I'm trying," Melody said with a sigh. "But how do you get someone who is so horrible to be a nicer person?"

"Another thing you need to figure out," JD said easily. He reached into his pocket and pulled out a pack of gum. "Wanna piece?"

"No," Melody said. "JD, couldn't you send Cisco or Nicole down to help me? Please?"

"It's up to the Big Guy," JD said with a shrug. He popped a stick of gum in his mouth. "I'm trying to quit smoking. It's a killer. Anyway, remember that I don't get to call the shots."

"Well, could you ask Him for me?" Melody begged. "Cisco is so cool—she could handle Scarlett. And Nicole is so smart, she'd figure out what to do. But me . . ."

"Hey, don't underestimate yourself!" JD said. He thought a minute. "There is one thing I could do to help you out . . ."

"What?" Melody asked eagerly.

"Well, usually I don't offer this particular little feature until the second or third Earth assignment, but maybe I can make an exception . . ."

"What? Tell me!" Melody exclaimed.

"It's called the Mega-Phone," JD explained. He hopped off the TV set and walked over to Melody. "What you do is you turn on the TV set. Go ahead, do it."

Melody got up, found the remote, and clicked on the TV.

"Now, click in this code," JD said. He handed her a piece of paper with a series of numbers on it.

Melody quickly clicked in all the numbers.

"This only works if you're alone, you understand," JD explained. "And it only works if you're a Teen Angel. Oh, and you're gonna be coughing up some major angel points when you get back home, but . . ."

Cisco and Nicole's faces appeared on the TV screen.

"It's Cisco and Nicole!" Melody cried with happiness.

"Mel?" Cisco said, peering out of the TV. "Wow, great robe!"

"This is fantastic!" Melody cried. "Oh, I miss you guys so much!"

"Pretty cool, huh?" JD said. "Better than a phone—that's why we call it a Mega-Phone. Anyway, you can only chat for five minutes, then the screen will go blank."

"Thank you so much, JD," Melody said. "I really—"

"Never hurry, never worry!" JD sang out. He snapped his fingers and disappeared.

"Whoa, this is totally amazing," Cisco said. "I can see the room you're in and everything!"

"It's called a Mega-Phone," Melody explained. "JD just showed me how to use it!"

"He has so many tricks up his sleeve," Nicole said with admiration. "So, how are you?"

"I'm okay, but I have so much to tell you guys," Melody said in a rush, "and I only have five minutes!"

"So, cut to the chase!" Cisco suggested.

"Okay," Melody said. "I hate my mission and I know I'm going to fail, and in an hour I have a date with a guy who is after me and I miss Chaz so much my heart hurts."

"What's the prob with the mission?" Cisco asked.

Melody quickly explained about Scarlett. "I feel so guilty!" she exclaimed. "What kind of an angel am I if I can't even find a way to like the girl I'm supposed to help?"

"Have you tried just totally telling her off?" Cisco said. "Maybe that would give her a clue."

"I could never do that!" Melody said, aghast. "For one thing, I'd never have the nerve!"

"Well, let's look at it logically," Nicole said. "She must be the way she is for a reason. You need to find out the reason, and then you can deal with the problem!"

"You think?" Melody asked doubtfully.

"Who cares why she's a creep?" Cisco asked. "Some girls are just born ugly on the inside!"

"No one is born ugly, Cisco," Nicole said. "Psychologists say that—"

"You guys!" Melody interrupted. "Please! I only have three minutes left!"

"You need to get closer to her," Nicole said firmly. "That's the only way."

"I'll try," Melody said with a sigh. "How's Chaz?"

"He misses you just as much as you miss him," Nicole reported.

"Really?" Melody asked dreamily.

"It's kind of disgusting how much he talks about you," Cisco teased. "That boy has got it bad."

"The more guys I meet on Earth, the more I appreciate Chaz," Melody said. "Listen, I need to know what you guys think about this. Am I cheating on Chaz if I go out with someone else while I'm on Earth?"

"For romance or as part of your mission?" Nicole asked.

"For my mission," Melody said firmly. "This guy is Scarlett's boyfriend's best friend. So then the four of us can do things together . . ."

"I say it's cool," Cisco decided. "Of course, you aren't allowed to have any actual *fun*—"

"I would never!" Melody insisted.

"I'm teasing you, Mel," Cisco said. "Dang, I wish I could see more of that house you're staying in. It looks great!"

"This is kind of a rich neighborhood," Melody said. "That's another thing. I don't know how to act around all these rich kids!"

"Just be yourself," Nicole advised.

"Oh, that statement just bites my angelic butt," Cisco snorted.

Melody laughed.

"Well, it does," Cisco said. "There's no book that can tell you who yourself should be. It's all just a bunch of bull!"

"So what should I do, then?" Melody asked with frustration.

"Whatever you feel like doing!" Cisco declared.

"There aren't any easy answers, Mel," Nicole said. "Believe me, I felt just as scared and insecure when I was down there."

"You did?" Melody asked faintly.

"I did, too," Cisco admitted. "And you're gonna do great, girlfriend. You know we believe in you!"

"Thanks," Melody said. "Thanks for believing in

me." She looked at the clock. "I only have one minute," she said quickly. "Tell me what's going on with everyone."

"Nicole and Jake are practically married," Cisco reported.

"She's exaggerating," Nicole said. "But we are . . . happy." She looked over at Cisco. "Cisco is thinking about going out with Jake's roommate—"

"That's great, Cisco!" Melody declared.

"Not so fast," Cisco said grumpily. "I'm still in my no-guys phase, okay?"

"Not for long, I predict," Nicole said.

The picture on the TV began to shimmer around the edges.

"Tell Chaz I love him!" Melody said quickly. "No, wait! Don't tell him that! Oh, my God, I can't even believe I said that! He'll think I'm crazy!"

"Our lips are sealed," Nicole promised. "We'll tell him you miss him—how's that?"

"Yes, tell him," Melody said. The picture began to dim. "I love you guys!"

"We love you, too, Mel!" Nicole called.

"And you're a Teen Angel, girl!" Cisco added. "You just remember that when the going gets tough!"

"I'll try!" Melody cried.

But she was talking to herself.

The TV had gone blank.

Six

"Table for four," Jeff told the maître d' at the restaurant.

The foursome waited as the maître d' looked for the reservation in the book. It was that evening, and Melody was out on her double date with Gray, Scarlett, and Jeff. Both Mrs. Snider and Cindy had told her how wonderful she looked when Gray came to the house to pick her up, but she felt nervous and guilty. She just couldn't accept that it was really okay for her to be going out on a date with someone other than Chaz, even if it was part of her mission.

"There's a thirty- to forty-minute wait," the maître d' told Jeff briskly.

"Are you sure?" Jeff asked.

"I told you you should have booked, man," Gray said with a sigh.

"Look, couldn't you move us to the front of the line or something?" Jeff asked.

"Why would I do that?" the maître d' asked, clearly not impressed that he was dealing with teenagers, even if they were rich and well dressed. "Like your friend said, you should have booked."

"Is Barry here?" Scarlett asked, flipping her long, honey-colored hair off her face.

"Barry?" the maître d' repeated blankly.

"Barry Clemence," Scarlett said. "Maybe you've heard of him. He owns this restaurant. And he's my godfather."

"Scarlett!" Barry said, who stopped before he rushed by. "I didn't know you were coming in tonight!"

"Hi, Uncle Barry," she said sweetly, kissing him on the cheek. "We're celebrating. I got the lead in the school play."

"Again," Barry added, a big grin on his handsome face.

"This guy must be new," Scarlett said, cocking her head toward the maître d'. "He just told me I have to wait a half hour for a table."

Barry turned to the maître d'. "Find them a table right away."

"Yes, sir!" the maître d' said quickly.

Barry pinched Scarlett's cheek. "Anything else you need, princess?"

"Not a thing!" Scarlett said gaily. "Thanks!"

"Right this way," the maître d' said, and they followed him to an intimate, well-placed booth near the large picture window.

"Is there anyone in Nashville you can't wrap around your finger?" Jeff asked as they sat down.

"What, did you want us to wait in line?" Scarlett asked snippily.

"Nope," Jeff said. "It just never fails to amaze me that you always manage to get your own way."

Scarlett shrugged. "So, tell us how gorgeous we look," she suggested.

"I don't need any coaxing to do that," Gray said, looking at Melody.

"Hello, I'm Nick. I'll be your waiter this evening," the thin, young waiter said, handing them the heavy, oversized embossed-leather menus. "We have a number of specials this evening, and I'd be happy to go over them for you." Nick launched into the list of specials, detailing how each one was prepared.

Wow, I've never even heard of half of the food he's talking about, Melody realized. I hope they actually have something I recognize, preferably without a messy sauce that I will undoubtedly spill all over myself.

"Would any of you care for a drink before you order?" Nick asked.

"We'll have champagne," Scarlett said imperiously. "Moet & Chandon would be fine."

"I'll need to see some ID," Nick said apologetically.

"Oh, please," Scarlett scoffed.

"I'm sorry, but the legal drinking age is twenty-one," Nick said. "I have to ask."

Scarlett gave a huge sigh. "Look, Barry Clemence—your boss—is my godfather. Now, if I want champagne, it's probably a good idea for you to serve us the champagne."

"Very good," Nick said, and he hurried off.

"You didn't need to be so rude to him," Jeff said mildly.

"I'm sick of being treated like a child," Scarlett snapped. "Besides, don't you think a drinking age is unbelievably hypocritical? Tell me one person at Whitmore that doesn't drink."

"Me," Melody said.

Scarlett stared at her. "You're kidding, right?"

"No, I really don't drink," Melody said. She thought about Cisco, and how she'd had to go into rehab and change her whole life because she had such a big problem with alcohol. "I saw a friend of mine get really messed up because of liquor, so . . . I guess that's why I don't."

"But sometime you just need to let loose and relax," Scarlett said.

"You don't relax," Jeff said, "you get wasted."

"What is this, 'pick on Scarlett night'?" she asked him. "Besides, I've seen you wasted plenty of times, too."

"Remember Roxanne Miller's party last year?" Gray asked. "Whoa, I thought my head was gonna fall off the next day."

"I can't even remember how many shots of tequila I did," Scarlett said. "And then we all jumped into her pool—"

"Who was that really scaggy girl from Hillsboro High who hurled in the pool?" Jeff asked.

"Oh, God, did you have to remind me?" Scarlett groaned.

"I'm sorry," Nick said, appearing once again at their table, "but I talked to Barry and he said that I can't serve you alcohol since you're under age. Would you like a Shirley Temple?"

Jeff cracked up and Scarlett gave him a murderous look. "Just forget it," she snapped. They all ordered their dinners. Melody had selected roast chicken, since she actually knew what that was. Nick hurried off with the menus.

"So, you can't always get everything you want!" Jeff hooted.

"If you keep it up, you won't get *anything* you want tonight," Scarlett told him nastily.

"Ha! She got you!" Gray laughed. He turned to Melody. "You okay?"

"Oh, I'm fine," she assured him.

"You're kind of quiet."

"I'm just listening," Melody said with a smile.

Gray put his arm around her. "You're sweet," he said.

Melody stiffened. She wanted to move Gray's arm, but she felt stupid. He didn't seem to notice at all how uncomfortable she was.

"Unlike someone else at this booth," Jeff teased Scarlett.

"Oh, shut up, Jeff," Scarlett said. She turned to Melody. "So, tell us about Detroit. It has to be more interesting than Nashville."

"There's not much to tell, really," Melody said.

"Oh, come on," Gray said. "I heard you were some kind of big model or something."

"Who said that?" Melody asked with surprise.

"Thunder Thighs, the Cheerleading Ogre," Scarlett said. "She's just *so* impressed with you. I guess it showed up on your records or something."

"I did some modeling," Melody admitted.

"You could get look-a-like work as Marilyn Monroe," Jeff said, his eyes scanning her body. "No lie."

"I don't think there's a big call for that, really," Melody said, nervous to be talking about herself.

"That is such a stupid idea," Scarlett told Jeff. "It's not like she needs the money."

"Why, are you rich like Scarlett?" Gray teased.

"Yeah, like your family isn't rich, too," Scarlett said.

Gray shrugged. "My dad is a doctor. That doesn't make us rich—at least not Whitmore rich."

"Scarlett has no idea how the other half lives," Jeff said.

"Ya'll can tease me all you want," Scarlett said coolly. "I don't care."

"Well, I'm not rich," Melody said in a small voice. "Not at all." She held her breath, hoping she was doing the right thing in admitting that she wasn't rich. Maybe I can get through to Scarlett that way, she thought to herself. Maybe one of her problems is that she just doesn't hang out with anyone who has to struggle.

"I thought you were," Scarlett said accusingly.

"No," Melody replied. "I never said I was."

"But your clothes," Scarlett said. "You wear designer stuff. Believe me, I know the difference."

"Uh . . . sometimes when I model I get to keep the clothes," Melody invented quickly. "I could never afford to buy the clothes I have."

"But models make a lot of money," Jeff protested. "Don't they?"

"Sometimes," Melody said. "But I had to support my family with my modeling jobs."

"Are your parents bums or something?" Scarlett asked disdainfully.

"They got divorced," Melody explained. "And then—"

"Oh, this is too boring and depressing," she interrupted. "We're supposed to be celebrating. Let's talk about how fantastic I'm going to be in the play. Oh, and Melody, too."

She proceeded to talk about all the cute outfits she was going to wear as Cherie. Melody sighed. Well, that episode of *True Confessions* was a total bust, she realized. Nothing I try seems to do any good at all. How can I possibly get through to Scarlett? How?

* * *

". . . So then Beth goes, 'You've been spreading all these lies about how I'm, like, doing it with every guy in school, right?' And then Shannon goes, 'Well, I only said that because you told Gray that I like him and I was totally humiliated . . .'"

From the backseat Melody sighed and stared out the window. They had finished a sumptuous dinner, and now they were heading back to Scarlett's house, where Melody had made plans to spend the night. Scarlett was telling yet another story about her friends—who was mad at, not speaking to, doing it, or was in love with whom.

I am bored to death, Melody thought to herself. *If this is what I missed out on by not going to high school on Earth my senior year, then I didn't miss much of anything.*

"Cold?" Gray asked, putting his arm around her, again.

"Oh, no, I'm fine," Melody assured him.

"So, how do you like Nashville so far?" Gray asked.

"It seems really nice," Melody said lamely.

"It's so hick," Gray snorted. "I can't stand it. We moved here from Los Angeles when I was ten. I can't wait to graduate and get out."

"Where do you want to go to school?" Melody asked politely.

"UCLA, maybe," Gray said. "That's where both my parents went. I think that means they have to take me or something. Where do you want to go?"

"Oh . . . I . . . haven't decided yet," Melody lied.

"You really should go to Hollywood and get into the movies," Gray said. He pulled her closer.

At that moment Jeff pulled the car down a dark side road.

"Is this a shortcut to Scarlett's?" Melody asked.

"I think you'd call it a detour," Gray said with a grin. He ran his fingers down her arm.

Jeff pulled the car up to a grove of trees at the edge of a small pond. He turned off the ignition. It was very dark and very quiet. He leaned over and opened the glove compartment and pulled out a fifth of Jack Daniels. "Ah, dessert!" he proclaimed.

"It's not exactly champagne, but it'll do," Scarlett said. She upended the bottle and took a long swallow—without choking—then she handed it to Jeff. He did the same and passed the bottle to the backseat.

"No, thanks," Melody said.

Gray shrugged and poured some whiskey into his mouth. "Oo, that's good, man," he said, exhaling loudly. He passed the bottle back to Jeff, then put his arm around Melody. She stiffened.

"Relax!" he said. "I'm not going to bite you!"

"Maybe she'd like that," Scarlett said, taking the bottle from Jeff. After she took another long pull at the bottle, she moved over and put her head on Jeff's shoulder. The next thing Melody knew Jeff and Scarlett were locked in a passionate embrace.

"Maybe we should go for a walk or something," Melody suggested.

"Good idea," Gray agreed, and they got out of the car. "Nice night, huh?"

"Beautiful," Melody agreed. "In Detroit it's already cold this time of year." She inhaled deeply. "The air smells great."

"So do you," Gray said. He put both arms around her neck.

73

"Uh, Gray . . ."

" 'Uh, Gray,' what?" he whispered, his voice teasing her.

"I told you before, I have a boyfriend," Melody said.

"So you did," he agreed. He ostentatiously looked to the right, then to the left. "He doesn't seem to be here right now."

"I know that," Melody said. "But, you know, it wouldn't be right . . ."

"Hey, you're not married," Gray pointed out. "You're young, you're fine, I'm reasonably fine myself, or so I'm told—so what's the problem?"

Melody took a tentative step away from him. "Well, you know, it's . . . I mean . . ." *Why don't you just assert yourself, you big wuss?* she wanted to scream at herself. *Just stand up for yourself! Just tell him you're not interested!*

"You're not gonna try telling me you just want us to be friends, are you?" Gray asked in that same teasing, confident voice. He reached out and ran his knuckles gently over her cheek.

"I don't want to hurt your feelings," Melody murmured.

Gray laughed. "Wow, I haven't heard that one before!"

"Because you've gotten every girl you ever wanted?" Melody asked.

"Yeah, to be honest, I have," Gray admitted. "I bet you've gotten every guy you ever wanted, too. Come on, admit it."

For a date, maybe, Melody thought. But as soon as they found out I wasn't going to put out, they moved on.

"Hey, are you about to be my first heartbreak?" Gray asked with a laugh.

"I'm sure I'm not breaking your heart," Melody said. "You don't even know me."

"That's what I'm trying to do," Gray said. "I'm trying to get to know you." He put his arms around her neck again and leaned down to kiss her.

"I'm sorry," Melody said, moving away again. I hate myself! she thought. Even though I know Gray is the one who is wrong, as usual I'm the one who feels guilty!

Gray laughed and ran his hand through his hair. "It's cool," he said easily. "I like a challenge."

"Maybe we should just go," Melody said nervously.

"Sure," Gray agreed. "I'm a patient guy. And I have a feeling you're worth waiting for."

They walked back over to the car. When Gray opened the door and the light went on inside the car, it illuminated Scarlett and Jeff in the backseat, their clothes in incredible disarray.

"Oops," Gray said, and shut the door again.

"Now what are we supposed to do?" Melody asked.

"The same thing they're doing?" Gray asked hopefully.

"Do you think you could ask them if we could leave?" Melody asked tentatively.

Gray laughed. "I don't think they're in a leaving kind of mood right about now," he pointed out.

Melody took a deep breath and made a decision. She went over to the car and knocked on the window.

"What?" Scarlett's muffled voice asked.

"I really want to go," Melody said firmly.

"*Now?*" Jeff asked.

"Yes," Melody said. "You two can drop me off at the Sniders if you want, and then come back out here." She wanted to add an "I'm sorry," but she forced herself to bite the words back.

"Oh, brother," Jeff groaned. "Okay, okay." Two minutes later they opened the car door and returned to the front seat; Melody and Gray climbed in back.

"What'd you do—strike out?" Jeff asked Gray as he started the car.

"Hey, so she's not a first-date kind of babe," Gray said. "I like a challenge."

"Take us to my house," Scarlett said. She pulled her brush out of her purse and began to brush her hair.

"Hey!" Jeff protested. "What about me?"

"What about you?" Scarlett asked. "Melody is spending the night at my house."

Jeff swore under his breath, but he drove them to Scarlett's house—mansion was more like it—and pulled the car up the huge circular driveway. "Are you inviting us in?" he asked hopefully.

"No," Scarlett said, getting out of the car. Melody grabbed the overnight case she'd put in the car, and she got out, too.

"Oh, so what am I supposed to do now?" Jeff demanded.

"You're supposed to say 'goodnight, girls!' " Scarlett said, then she blew Jeff a kiss.

Gray got out of the car and stood next to Melody. "So, I'll see you soon," he promised.

"Thanks for dinner," Melody said. "It was really nice."

Gray leaned over and kissed her softly before she could protest. "Soon," he promised, then he got into the front seat next to Jeff. Jeff pulled away with a squeal of the tires and raced the car down the street.

"That is so juvenile," Scarlett said as they went into the house. "Welcome to my happy home."

Melody stood in the center of a huge, circular hall that ran three stories to a cathedral-like ceiling. There was thick, white carpeting everywhere. Various works of art, including large sculptures, were displayed in a room off the hall to the right. To the left, down some steps, was a vast living room, with modern white furniture arranged artfully in the room. Above the couch was a huge oil painting of a woman who looked like Scarlett, but older. Melody looked up. A giant crystal chandelier hung over her head.

"It's . . . unbelievable," Melody murmured faintly.

"Ugh," Scarlett said. She cocked her head toward the room filled with art. "Mother's gallery," she explained. "She collects young artists' work before they become famous. Or maybe she collects the artists, I forget."

Melody had no idea what Scarlett meant, so she didn't say anything.

"Oh, good evening, Miss Whitmore," said an older woman in a black maid's uniform, as she walked into the entrance hall.

"Hi, Hildy," Scarlett said. "This is my friend, Melody."

"Hello," Hildy said.

"Hildy has worked for my family forever," Scarlett explained. "Where's Mom and Dad?"

"Your mother is in the family room, your father is still at the office," Hildy reported.

"Yeah, I bet," Scarlett said. "We might as well go in so you can meet my mother," she told Melody. "She'll have a fit tomorrow if I don't introduce you tonight." She turned to Hildy. "Is she—?"

Hildy shrugged. "I haven't been in the family room for hours. Sorry."

"Might as well face the music," Scarlett said with a sigh. "Come on."

"It was nice to meet you," Melody told Hildy, then she hurried after Scarlett down a hallway that led to a large, pine-panelled room with floor-to-ceiling bookshelves lining an entire wall. All the books there were leather-bound. A large-screen TV dominated one wall. Mounted on another wall, over a huge fireplace, were several stuffed animal heads. Melody shuddered and looked away.

Sitting in a maroon leather chair was a beautiful, slender woman with the same honey-blonde hair as Scarlett's, only hers was swept back in a perfect chignon at the back of her head. She looked to be in her mid-forties. She wore impeccable cream wool trousers with a cream-colored cashmere sweater and a single strand of perfect pearls. She was leafing through a book of photos and sipping from a glass.

"Hi, Mom," Scarlett said. She plopped down on the couch.

"Look at this," Scarlett's mother said, turning a page in the book of photographs. "Just look at this. I haven't gained an ounce since the year I married your father."

Scarlett rolled her eyes. "Mom, this is Melody. Remember I told you she was coming over to spend the night?"

"Oh, God, I remember this," Scarlett's mother said, still staring at the book of photos. She picked up her drink and took a sip. "It was the first dance we went to together at the country club. I ordered that dress from Paris . . ."

"Mom, the house is burning down and I'm pregnant with *Elvis'* love child," Scarlett said.

Mrs. Whitmore finally looked up. "I hated Elvis," she said blankly. "All that disgusting pompadoured hair." She drained her glass and held it out to Scarlett. "Make me another, dear."

Melody realized that Scarlett's mother was drunk because she was just slightly slurring her words.

"Why, how lovely to meet my darling daughter Scarlett's new friend," Scarlett said, imitating what she wished her mother would have said. She took the glass from her mother and walked over to the bar in the corner.

Mrs. Whitmore finally looked over at Melody. She stared at her for a long moment. "You're awfully pretty," she finally said, but she made it sound like an accusation, not a compliment.

"Thank you," Melody said, since she didn't know what else to say.

"It doesn't last," Mrs. Whitmore said in a flat voice. "Keep that in mind."

"Yes, I will," Melody said.

"Scarlett is very attractive," Mrs. Whitmore said. "However, most of that comes from youth. All she'll end up is old and ugly, I'm afraid."

Melody couldn't help it—she gasped out loud.

"Ignore her," Scarlett advised, pouring her mother some more bourbon. "It's the drinks talking."

"No woman is beautiful over the age of forty," Mrs. Whitmore said, as if she hadn't heard her daughter at all. "We all end up old and ugly." She gave her daughter a cool, appraising look. "Is that a new outfit?"

"You noticed!" Scarlett said.

"It doesn't flatter you," Mrs. Whitmore said. "Are you putting on weight?"

"No," Scarlett said. Her voice was beginning to sound irritated.

"I think we need to find a new hairdresser for you," she said, still appraising her daughter. "Your hair looks dry."

"Okay, so I'm a pig with a haystack on my head—anything else?" Scarlett said lightly. She handed her mother a fresh drink.

"You're not fat, Scarlett," Mrs. Whitmore said, sipping her drink. "Not yet, anyway. But you do need to watch it. Once you let yourself go, it's all over."

"We're going up to—" Scarlett began.

"What was that?" Mrs. Whitmore asked sharply, listening keenly.

"I didn't hear anything," Scarlett said.

"I thought it might be your father . . ."

"He's working late," Scarlett said sarcastically.

"It doesn't matter to me," Mrs. Whitmore said, taking a large gulp of her fresh drink. "I happen to have a meeting tomorrow with a new young artist. He's twenty-two. How old is your father's secretary?"

"I don't know," Scarlett said.

"Older than twenty-two," Mrs. Whitmore said smugly. She turned and narrowed her eyes at her daughter. "Never trust a man, Scarlett. You remember that. They all stink."

"Thank you for that motherly advice," Scarlett said. "We're going up to my room now. 'Bye."

"Oh, look how young I am in this photo . . ." Mrs. Whitmore was saying as the girls left the room.

They scampered up the circular stairway, down a hall, and into a huge room, which belonged to Scarlett. An antique four-poster bed dominated the room, which was beautifully decorated with antiques. A collection of Raggedy Anne dolls was perched on a rosewood trunk in the corner. "Alone at last," Scarlett said, throwing herself on the bed. "Isn't my mother a hoot?"

"Does she . . . have a drinking problem?" Melody asked hesitantly.

"Does a bear have fur?" Scarlett asked. "I mean, really, what was your first clue?"

Melody blushed. "She just seems so unhappy . . ."

"Yes, poor dear, she suffers so," Scarlett said melodramatically. "All she has is millions, beauty, brains, health. How can she stand it?"

"Maybe she needs to . . . I don't know . . . see a therapist or something," Melody suggested tentatively. She sat on the edge of Scarlett's bed.

"Been there, done that," Scarlett sang out. "Believe me, Mom has been dried-out by the best. She's just totally obsessed with the fact that she's getting older and losing her looks. She's had four facelifts already, and she's only forty-four!"

"Your parents don't get along?" Melody asked.

Scarlett laughed bitterly. "They get along great, because they never see each other! Dad does the secretary, Mom does whichever young artist is her current 'find,' and everyone lives happily ever after!"

"I'm really sorry," Melody said.

"I'm not," Scarlett said, jumping up from the bed. "As long as they stay out of my hair, why should I care?" She reached behind her and unzipped the top to her outfit and pulled it over her head.

"Because they're your parents," Melody said.

Scarlett stepped out of her new skirt and carelessly kicked it under the bed.

81

"I'm sure you love them," Melody began tentatively.

"I guess," Scarlett said, sounding bored with the world. "Want to smoke a joint or something?"

"No, thanks," Melody said. "You know, there's this organization called Al-anon, have you ever heard of it? When you have an alcoholic in your family you can—"

"Look, it's my mother's problem, not mine," Scarlett said sharply. She pulled an oversized sweatshirt from her drawer and pulled it over her head.

"Scarlett?" It was Hildy, standing in the doorway.

"What?"

"I have a surprise for you," Hildy said, a grin on her face. "Guess who got back from the animal hospital a day early?"

"Pickles!" Scarlett screamed with joy.

Into the room ran a beautiful chocolate-brown cocker spaniel with floppy ears and soulful eyes. He was absolutely darling, but Melody noticed that he ran with a pronounced limp. Still he made it over to Scarlett as fast as his legs would carry him, and he leaped into her arms and covered her face with doggy kisses.

"Oh, Pickles!" Scarlett cried, hugging the dog tightly. "I missed you so much!"

"I knew you'd be happy," Hildy said. "Good night."

"Thanks, Hildy!" Scarlett called after the woman. She turned the dog to Melody. "Pickles, I want you to meet Melody. Melody, this is my best friend, Pickles, the wonder dog!"

"Hi, there," Melody said, giving Pickles a scratch under her chin. "What a beauty you are!"

"Oh, Pickles, I love you so much!" Scarlett said, kissing the dog on her nose.

Pickles scrambled down and limped around the room, her tail wagging wildly.

"What happened to her leg?" Melody asked. "Did she have an accident?"

"No, she was born without a hip socket in one of her hind legs," Scarlett explained. "When I was ten I begged my parents to get me a dog. I mean, I was always rattling around this mausoleum by myself. They're never home. So my mom said okay, as long as it was beautiful, didn't clash with the decor, and had a perfect pedigree. So we went to the breeders and there were these new puppies. They cost a lot of money. But they were planning to send Pickles to the pound. Because of her limp. She wasn't perfect so she wasn't worth anything."

"And you picked her . . ." Melody said, her voice full of wonder.

Scarlett nodded as Pickles jumped into her arms again. "We picked each other. She was just as good as the other dogs. I didn't tell my mother about the limp. And I made her pay the breeder the full price for the dog, too, even though they would have given Pickles away for free."

"Why did you pick her?" Melody asked.

"Because I know what it feels like to not be perfect enough," Scarlett said fiercely. "I know just exactly how it feels."

Seven

"Okay, everyone," Ms. Russell said, lifting her glasses off her long nose and pushing them up to an extremely precarious perch on top of her forehead, "let's take our dinner break now. We'll resume later."

"Take an hour!" Corky McGee called in a loud voice. She was sitting next to Ms. Russell, at the long director's table in front of the stage. "Back at seven o'clock and we'll go until eight-thirty!"

It was Monday, after school, and rehearsals for *Bus Stop* were in full swing. They took priority over everything for the kids who were in the cast, including cheerleading practice. Miss Sunder wasn't too happy about that, but there was nothing she could do about it.

Ms. Russell had quickly blocked the play—basically telling the actors where they were supposed to move on stage—and she was now moving forward into actual character work.

Melody walked off the stage, thankful to be taking a break. She hadn't slept well the night before; she just had too much on her mind.

She kept playing her evening with Scarlett over and over in her mind. Just when it seemed as if Scarlett was going to let Melody in, she had shut down again.

Once I saw what Scarlett's mom is like, and once I met Pickles, I got a totally different impression of Scarlett, Melody thought to herself. Oh, she's still just as obnoxious as ever, but now at least I see where it's coming from. The problem is, I think she needs a really good therapist or something, not a Teen Angel who barely finished high school!

"You're doing a really good job," said a nice girl named Carol from Melody's English class, as she reached for a can of red paint to help paint pieces of the set, which were scattered around in the theater. "I heard you were, like, this big professional actress in Detroit or something."

"Not at all!" Melody protested. "I don't even have any talent!"

"Oh, sure," the girl said, laughing as she walked away.

Melody reached into her purse and took out the banana she'd brought along as a snack. She ate it quickly, wishing she'd brought more food. I am still starving, she thought ruefully. Acting is hard work! She put her hands on her stomach, doing her usual check to see if she seemed any fatter. It was second nature to her. Out of the corner of her eye she caught sight of Corky eating a small package of cheese and crackers.

"Yo, Porky, what'd ya bring to eat on the break, a few gallons of ice cream?" called out a guy painting scenery.

"Yum, yum," grunted his friend, and the two of them laughed together.

"You guys are so mean," Carol told them as she

wiped off her paintbrush. "All she's eating is that little tiny package of cheese and crackers. Maybe she's trying to lose weight."

Corky finished her snack and Melody watched her walk backstage, ignoring the idiots who were laughing at her. Just then Scarlett walked up to Melody, and she was scowling.

"Look, I know what you're pulling and it won't work," Scarlett snapped, her hands on her hips.

"What are you talking about?"

"Pretend you don't know," Scarlett sneered.

"I don't," Melody said in a small voice, feeling very intimidated.

"Yeah, right," Scarlett said bitterly. "You can forget about us coming over later."

"Why?" Melody asked softly, dumbfounded.

This was bad news. Earlier in the day, Scarlett had made plans for her, Jeff, and Gray to come over to the Sniders's to hang out with Melody for a while when rehearsal was over.

"Listen, don't ever do that to me again."

"Do what?" Melody asked, feeling upset. "I don't know what you're talking about!"

"Right," Scarlett said. "Just because you're this big model and actress doesn't mean you can come in here and upstage me. Don't ever try that again, Melody Monroe. Or you'll be really sorry." And with those words, Scarlett turned and walked toward the back of the auditorium.

"What in the world is 'upstaging'?" Melody asked in a loud voice, truly distressed.

Scarlett stopped as she heard Melody's question from over her shoulder. She turned around slowly. "You're kidding . . ."

Melody shrugged blankly.

"I thought you were supposed to be this big professional—"

"Look, I never said that!" Melody exclaimed. "Someone started that rumor but it just isn't true!"

"Okay, I'll forgive you," Scarlett said decisively, walking slowly toward Melody. "*This time.*"

"But what did I do?"

"You kept going up the stage, away from the audience," Scarlett explained. "So I kept having to turn my back to the audience. It's called *upstaging.*"

"But—"

"Just don't do it anymore, okay?" Scarlett commanded. "Anyway, I'll see you later. Jeff's waiting for me outside."

With that, she hurried out of the auditorium, and Melody shook her head helplessly.

Ms. Russell directed me to go upstage then, Melody had been about to say to Scarlett. *Not that it would have done any good to tell you.*

She sighed and sat down, feeling lonely, confused, and utterly frustrated. I'm not getting anywhere with Scarlett at all, she thought. I might as well admit it. So what if I know the truth about her terrible home life? I don't see how that's going to help me help her! Maybe I'm just not Teen Angel material.

Melody got up and headed for the girls' bathroom. As soon as she opened the bathroom door, she stopped in shock.

Someone was in the stalls, behind a closed door, making horrible noises. The sounds of violent retching and vomiting echoed off the tiles of the bathroom.

Deep Six, Melody thought frantically, panicking. *It's someone from Deep Six.* The Bad Dude sent someone to interfere with my mission! And that someone's in there! It happened with Cisco, it happened with Nicole, and now it's going to happen to me!

The door to a stall swung open. Melody stood rock-still, frozen with fear.

Out came Corky McGee.

"What are you staring at?" Corky asked Melody, her voice full of hostility.

"Thank God," Melody said quickly, "it's you."

"Who did you think it was, the boogeyman?" Corky sneered, but tears were starting to fill her eyes.

"Yes!" Melody blurted out, even though she knew Corky wouldn't have a clue as to what she was talking about.

And then Corky slumped down on the tiles of the bathroom floor, crying as hard as Melody had ever seen anyone cry.

Melody took a quick look at the bathroom door. There was no way she could lock it and protect Corky's privacy. She said a quick prayer that no one would come in, and then, respectfully, approached the bawling girl who everyone ragged on all the time.

She was making herself throw up, Melody realized. She was doing it as a way to try to lose weight. If only she knew . . .

"Don't tell," Corky moaned, her voice wracked by sobs. "Don't tell anyone."

"I won't tell," Melody said softly, sitting down on the cold tiles next to Corky.

"Please," Corky said, her voice cracking with the sobs, "don't tell."

"I will never tell," Melody said again, her voice even softer. "You can trust me."

"Ha!" Corky sniffed, tears flowing down her face. "You're friends with Scarlett Whitmore."

Melody could easily figure out what Corky was

thinking. If Scarlett Whitmore were to find out that Corky was eating and throwing up, Melody reasoned, the whole school would find out by the time class started tomorrow. Corky's life would be even more of a living hell than it is right now. As if that were humanly possible.

"God, I hate my life!" Corky cried. "I want to die!"

"Believe it or not, I understand how you feel," Melody said softly.

"Yeah, right," Corky said, shuddering from her sobs. "You really know what it's like to have people make fun of you every day. Every single day! I want to kill them, I hate them all so much!" More tears began to flow down her face. "You know what I do? I hardly eat anything in front of them, because I think maybe they won't pick on me so much if they don't see me eat. But just now in the stall I ate five candy bars. And then I made myself throw them all up. God, I'm so disgusting!" She doubled over with sobs, holding her stomach and rocking back and forth.

Melody grabbed some tissues from her purse and handed them to Corky. "I really do understand," Melody said.

"Oh, please," Corky sniffled, wiping her eyes. "You're gorgeous. You're perfect. You haven't got a clue."

"Yes, I do," Melody said. "You're not the only one who eats and then throws up."

Corky blew her nose, then gave Melody an appraising look. "You mean you do it too?" she cried, her voice full of wonder.

"*Used* to do it," Melody admitted. "For all of the ninth grade. My mom ragged on me all the time, she was so afraid I'd get fat and I wouldn't be able to model. She weighed me three times a day."

"For real?" Corky asked, blowing her nose again.

"Yes," Melody said. "It was my dirty little secret. I felt really ashamed. Anyway, if I tell anyone about you," Melody continued, "you tell them about me."

Corky nodded slowly. "I can't believe you did this too," she said. "How did you stop?"

"I'll tell you all about it," Melody said, getting up slowly to her feet. "If you want."

Corky looked up at Melody. "I hate me," she said slowly. "I totally hate me."

"I've hated me, too," Melody said, extending her right hand down to Corky. "But let's talk about it someplace else, not here, okay?"

Corky stared up at Melody, who continued to hold out her hand. And then, very slowly, Corky took Melody's hand and got to her feet, not even thinking about letting go.

Ding-dong!

The front door bell at the Sniders's house sounded, and Melody hurried to get it, sneaking a quick look at her watch. It was nine-thirty, play rehearsal had ended an hour earlier, and she still had a fair amount of homework to finish.

They can only stay about forty-five minutes or so, she thought as she went to answer the door, expecting to see Jeff, Gray, and Scarlett together. It's not fair that I have to do both Teen Heaven High homework and Whitmore High homework!

"Hey," Gray said easily, as Melody opened the door. "You look great!"

"I'm wearing jeans and a sweatshirt!" Melody said with a laugh.

"You sure are," Gray added, his voice full of innuendo.

Melody smiled politely and ushered in the two boys, but once inside she was thinking that there was something about Gray and his insinuations that really, really rubbed her the wrong way.

"Scarlett left a message on my machine saying she was driving over herself," Jeff said, as the two guys followed Melody into the Sniders's kitchen. Mr. and Mrs. Snider were tactfully upstairs, and they'd ordered Cindy to stay out of the way while Melody's friends were visiting.

"Can I get you some juice?" Melody asked, going to the refrigerator and opening it.

"Cool," Jeff said, sitting down at the kitchen table.

"So you, like, live here?" Gray asked.

"Temporarily," Melody said, taking a pitcher of juice out of the fridge.

Just then the doorbell sounded again.

"I'll get it," Melody said. "Excuse me." She went through the hallway to the front door, saw through the glass that it was Scarlett, and opened it.

"Hi, Scarlett," Melody began. "Everyone's—"

"Where is that jerk?" Scarlett snarled, pushing her way past Melody into the house. "I'll kill him!" She stormed through the hallway into the kitchen, with Melody following close behind.

Now what, Melody sighed. She stared up at the ceiling. This girl is completely impossible. JD, can't you do something? JD didn't answer.

"You cretin," Scarlett said, spotting Jeff in the kitchen. "How dare you!"

"How dare I what?" Jeff responded, a look of complete bewilderment on his face.

"You know what I'm talking about," Scarlett said angrily, marching up to within a foot of Jeff's face.

"No, I don't," Jeff said quickly.

"Oh, sure," Scarlett said, her voice going up an octave. "Two-timing me!"

Melody thought a look of guilt crossed Jeff's face. Then, it quickly disappeared.

"What are you talking about?" Jeff demanded again.

Scarlett turned to Melody. "Ashley Daniels, who goes to Harpeth Hall, told me that Caitlin Morrell at Hume-Fogg told her she saw Jeff practically doing it with Jennifer Bogosian after the Hume-Fogg game."

"It's not true," Jeff defended himself. "I hardly know her!"

"Look, I know Jennifer Bogosian," Scarlett cried. "Half of Nashville knows her. She's a total slut."

"She is not," Jeff replied.

"Well, then why don't you just call her and let her tell me it's not true," Scarlett ordered Jeff.

Jeff looked down at his own shoes. "Okay, I will," he said, without much enthusiasm. "But I don't even know her number."

"Look it up," Scarlett said testily, tossing Jeff a Nashville phone directory that was by the kitchen telephone. "It's Bogosian. B-O-G-O—"

"I know how to spell her name!" Jeff yelled.

"What are you so upset about?" Scarlett screamed, so loudly that Melody quickly closed the door to the kitchen so that the Sniders wouldn't hear. "You're the one who's two-timing me!"

Jeff angrily threw the phone book back at Scarlett's feet. "Why don't you call her yourself?" he shot back.

Scarlett picked it up and started scanning pages,

running her finger down the columns of names and numbers. "Okay," she said, nastily, "I will."

Melody watched amazed as Scarlett found the number she wanted, picked up the kitchen wall phone, and quickly, angrily, punched in seven numbers.

"May I please speak with Jennifer Bogosian?" she said, in her sweetest voice, when someone on the other end answered her call.

Melody looked over at Jeff. His face was bright red. "Man," he mumbled, "this bites . . ."

"Jennifer?" Scarlett said into the phone. "Do you know who this is?"

Silence.

"A friend, Jennifer," Scarlett said, her voice still sweet. "No, it's not Carol Williams." She waited a moment. "No, not Katy Ann Gilchrist," Scarlett continued sweetly. Then her voice changed. "It's Scarlett Whitmore, you little two-timing witch . . ."

Scarlett stood there for a moment, the phone in her hand. Jennifer Bogosian had clearly hung up on her. She slammed the phone into the cradle.

"Look, she's lying—" Jeff began.

"No, she isn't," Scarlett said in a flat voice. "I can tell. So just stop lying to me."

The room was so quiet you could hear the clock ticking on the wall.

"We'll talk about this privately when you calm down," Jeff finally said, getting up. "You're, like, totally hysterical for no reason."

"Get out, Jeff, just get out," Scarlett said, her jaw set.

Jeff and Gray walked out without saying a word.

Melody sat down next to Scarlett. "I'm really sorry, Scarlett," she said quietly.

Scarlett looked down at her hands. "I . . . I thought

he really cared about me. I just can't believe he did that to me. No guy ever cheated on me before. I was always the one who cheated on them."

"I know it hurts," Melody said. She hesitated a moment. "I guess now you know how all those guys felt, huh?"

Scarlett didn't seem to hear her. "My mother is right," she said. "Men are terrible."

"That's not true—"

Scarlett looked at Melody, her face panicky. "You won't tell anyone about this, will you?"

"No, of course not."

"Because my rep would be shot," Scarlett said. "Can you imagine how much everyone would laugh at me?"

"It hurts when people laugh at you," Melody said, desperately trying to get through to Scarlett.

"Yeah . . ." Scarlett agreed, staring at her hands again.

Here's my big chance to get through to her, Melody thought.

"Since you know how much it hurts to be laughed at, maybe you won't laugh at anyone else anymore."

Scarlett looked up, and Melody was surprised to see tears streaming down her face. "It's because I'm just not perfect enough, right? That's why Jeff two-timed me . . ."

Melody sighed heavily. Because it was clear to her that as hurt as Scarlett was, the only pain she was concerned with was her own.

Eight

"Look, Melody, just because Jeff and Scarlett are history is no reason that we can't hang out," Gray said, as he walked Melody to her English class the next morning.

"But Gray, I told you," Melody said, "I already have a boyfriend."

"But he's there and you're here," Gray said easily. "And I'm here. With you."

"I just can't—"

"Sure you can," Gray insisted. They stopped right next to the door of the English class. Gray put his hand over Melody's shoulder on the wall and leaned toward her. "I'm not giving up, you know. I don't know how to take no for an answer."

Well, I wish you'd learn, Melody thought to herself.

"Hi, Gray," Scarlett's friend Jennifer said as she sailed by them.

"I have to go to class now," Melody said.

"I'll see you at lunch," Gray promised.

Once she entered Melody took her seat. Scarlett came in and sat next to her. "I am so ticked off," she told Melody and Jennifer, who was sitting on the other side of her.

"Why?" Melody asked.

"Just because I broke up with Jeff doesn't mean he should be going out with someone else the very next day," Scarlett said. "I heard he asked out Vicky Messinger."

"She's not even cute!" Jennifer exclaimed. "Why did you break up with Jeff, anyway?"

"I got sick of him," Scarlett said carelessly. She shot Melody a look of warning. "He's just so immature, don't you think? He doesn't even kiss that great. Finally, I had to cut him loose. He practically begged me not to break up with him. It was really pathetic, right, Melody?"

"Mmmm," mumbled Melody, looking down at her notebook. I know I said I wouldn't tell what really happened, Melody thought to herself, but there's no way I'm going to lie for her!

"You ought to go after Gray," Jennifer suggested. "He is so fine."

"I wouldn't want to steal him away from Melody," Scarlett said, tossing her head.

"I'm not going out with Gray!" Melody protested.

"It would make Jeff so totally jealous," Jennifer said.

"I couldn't care less," Scarlett said coolly. "I am totally over Jeff Walker."

The bell rang and Dr. Capelli stood up. "Okay, people, let's settle down."

"He always says that," Scarlett whispered to Melody. "Do you think he's some kind of robot?"

"Was there something you wanted to share with the class, Miss Whitmore?"

"If there was something I wanted to share with the

class, I would have said it out loud instead of whispering it, wouldn't I?'' Scarlett asked sweetly.

Dr. Capelli shook his head ruefully and began to write on the blackboard. ''Today we're going to discuss the difference between simile and metaphor,'' he said as he wrote. ''And you will all be writing papers showing usage of both.''

Melody dutifully opened her notebook and got out her pen. She began to copy everything down that Dr. Capelli was writing on the board.

More hours of homework, probably, she thought. I'm doomed.

She looked up to copy down the rest of what Dr. Capelli had written, and her heart practically leapt out of her mouth.

Because standing there next to Dr. Capelli was none other than Chaz Denton. *Her* Chaz Denton. From Teen Heaven.

But it can't be! Melody thought. Maybe I'm just hallucinating because I wish he was here so much. But there he is!

Chaz handed Dr. Capelli a pink slip from the office, then he turned and made eye contact with Melody.

And he gave her the sweetest smile in the world.

''Okay, people,'' Dr. Capelli said, ''it looks like we have another visiting student from Detroit joining us today. This is Chaz Denton. Chaz, you can take that last empty seat in the back row.''

''Chaz!'' Melody exclaimed.

''He's pretty cute,'' Scarlett said, sizing Chaz up. ''You know him?''

Melody laughed. ''He's my—''

But at the moment Chaz was about to walk by Melody's desk, he gave her a warning look, shaking his head just slightly.

"He's your what?" Scarlett asked.

"I . . . I know him," Melody said, totally confused. It had seemed to her that Chaz was warning her not to say he was her boyfriend. But why?

The seconds ticked by with agonizing slowness, until finally the bell rang and class was out.

Melody stood up, staring at Chaz.

"Introduce us," Scarlett demanded.

"He's cute," Jennifer added.

Chaz walked over. "Hi," he said easily.

Melody felt completely confused. "Hi, Chaz," she said in a stilted voice. "This is Scarlett Whitmore and Jennifer Powter."

"Nice to meet you," Chaz said. "Melody and I know each other from Mumford High in Detroit," he explained.

Melody tried to smile and act as if everything was normal. Why wasn't she allowed to say that Chaz was her boyfriend? What was going on?

Oh, Chaz, she thought, her heart breaking, *don't you care about me anymore?*

"So, how long will you be in Nashville?" Jennifer asked Chaz.

"A while," he said. "It seems pretty nice here."

"It isn't," Scarlett assured him. "Of course, if you know the right people, it's not all that bad."

Chaz laughed. "So how do I meet the right people?"

"Oh, I might be able to help you out," Scarlett said flirtatiously. She tossed her hair and gave Chaz a sexy smile. "What's your next class?"

"Art History," Chaz said.

"Oh, Melody's in that class," Scarlett said. "Well, I'll see you later, Chaz."

"Count on it," Chaz agreed. He watched Scarlett and Jennifer walk away.

Finally Melody and Chaz were alone in the classroom.

"Chaz?" Melody asked uncertainly.

Chaz carefully looked at the door to make sure no one was coming, then he took Melody in his arms. "Oh, Mel," he said, pulling her close. "Oh, God, I missed you so much . . ."

"But . . . but why wasn't I supposed to tell them you're my boyfriend?" Melody asked. "Why were you flirting with Scarlett?"

"JD sent me down to help you, Mel—" Chaz began. "But . . . it's hard to explain."

"Please," Melody said. "I have to know what's going on."

"Well, he sent me down to help you with Scarlett," Chaz said. "But—this is really hard—the way I'm supposed to help is that I'm supposed to start dating Scarlett."

"You're *what*?" Melody cried.

"Believe me," Chaz said, "I protested, too. But JD says that if you're her bud and I'm dating her, maybe between the two of us we'll make some progress with her."

"But . . . but you can't!" Melody exploded, tears in her eyes. "You just can't!"

"Mel," Chaz said, pulling her close again. "It won't mean a thing. I promise. Think of it as acting, okay?"

"But it will be so horrible!" Melody said.

"I know," Chaz agreed. "Don't you know how much I want to be with you?"

"I don't know anything," Melody admitted, brushing the tears off her cheeks.

"Mel, I . . . care about you a lot," Chaz said gruffly. "Just remember, for us this isn't real life. Okay?"

"I'll try," Melody said.

The rest of the day was agony for Melody. Every time she turned around it seemed as if she saw Scarlett with Chaz. And everytime Scarlett saw Jeff, she would wrap herself around Chaz ostentatiously.

I want to kill her, Melody thought. I want to snatch every hair out of her head. No. I can't think that way. This doesn't mean anything. Chaz doesn't care about her. That's what I have to remember. But it's so hard . . .

Right before play rehearsal was going to start, Chaz came into the theater and casually took a seat near the back. Scarlett immediately went back there and sat next to him, giggling and fooling around with him.

I won't look back there, Melody vowed to herself. *I just simply won't look.*

But she couldn't help herself. And what she saw twisted her heart. Chaz had his arm around Scarlett. He was pulling her close. He gave her a quick little kiss on the lips.

He hasn't even kissed me yet, she thought sadly. *JD, how could you do this to me?*

"Hi," Corky said, taking a seat next to Melody. "How are you?"

"Terrible," Melody said.

"How could someone who looks like you feel terrible?" Corky asked. Melody blinked the tears from her eyes and Corky saw how truly miserable Melody was. "Hey, I'm sorry," Corky said quickly. "Is there anything I can do?"

"No, but thanks," Melody said, gulping hard.

"Attention, please!" Ms. Russell called out to the group. "As you know, we open a week from Friday. It will be here before you know it. But some of you are still having trouble with your lines. That is simply inexcusable."

Everyone knew she meant Scarlett. Whenever an actor didn't know a line during rehearsal they were supposed to call out "line" and Corky, the stage manager, would give them the first few words of the line they missed. Not only did Scarlett call out "line" all the time, but she would turn to Corky and say, "What is it again?"—time and time again.

"Off book means off book," Ms. Russell said firmly. "There will be no calling for line from this rehearsal forward. If you get in hot water during the run-through, just get yourself out of it somehow. Everyone got that?"

From the back of the theater Scarlett giggled, and everyone turned around. She was playing some kind of game with Chaz and their fingers were intertwined.

"Scarlett," Ms. Russell called. "Do you think you could join us?"

"Yeah, sure," Scarlett said. She leaned over and whispered something in Chaz's ear, then she languidly walked down to the front and took a seat on the other side of Melody.

"Your friend is so cute," Scarlett whispered to Melody.

Melody tried to smile, but it was really, really hard.

As Ms. Russell droned on and on about the play, Scarlett leaned over to talk with Melody. "Don't you think Chaz will make Jeff crazy?"

"I don't think you should play those kind of games," Melody hissed at Scarlett. "They're stupid and juvenile."

"Well, get you!" Scarlett exclaimed, clearly taken aback.

A student came in and handed Ms. Russell a note, which she read quickly. "Excuse me, everyone, I'll be right back. Please run your lines while you're waiting."

Melody peeked at Chaz, who was still lolling in the back of the theater. "Listen, Chaz is a really nice guy," Melody said. "Don't use him."

"I'm not . . . exactly," Scarlett said insolently. "I think he's cute. I'm going out with him tonight. I'll bet he kisses great . . ."

"Do you ever think of anyone but yourself?" Melody exploded before she could stop herself.

"Come again?" Scarlett said coldly.

"I mean, what if Chaz has a girlfriend? Did you ever think of that?" Melody asked.

"What's your problem?" Scarlett demanded coldly.

"You're her problem," Corky said from the other side of Melody. "Maybe she's just as sick of you as I am."

"Well, I'll just leave you with your new best bud, Porky," Scarlett sneered. "I hope the two of you are happy together." She got up and moved far away from them.

"That was great!" Corky exulted.

"No, no, it was horrible," Melody moaned, putting her head in her hands.

"But you told off Scarlett Whitmore!" Corky said. "And I actually helped! And look! The world didn't come to an end!"

"Oh, God," Melody moaned. She got up quickly and ran toward the ladies' room. Corky ran after her.

"What? What is it?" Corky asked, as Melody sobbed into a hunk of toilet tissue.

"I've ruined everything!" Melody sobbed. "How could I say that to Scarlett?"

"Are you kidding?" Corky asked. "It was fantastic! I totally misjudged you, you know. You're not like Scarlett and her crowd at all."

"But she'll never even speak to me again!" Melody wailed.

"So? Who cares?" Corky asked. "You can't let it be that important to you to be in with the 'in' crowd. I mean, they are just so superficial and—"

"It isn't that," Melody interrupted. "It's . . . I can't explain it to you." She took a deep breath and tried to stop crying. "Let's just say that right now I'm letting everyone down. Including myself."

"Well, you're not letting me down," Corky said shyly.

"Thanks," Melody said, managing a small smile. "Oh, I brought you a book."

"What is it?" Corky asked.

"You asked me how I got myself to stop throwing up as a way of controlling my weight," Melody said, blowing her nose. "Well, I brought you a book about how I did it. It's in my backpack. I'll give it to you later."

"That's really nice of you," Corky said. "Say, you wouldn't want to go to the movies with me tonight, would you?"

"I don't think I feel up to it," Melody said, blowing her nose again.

"Yeah, I didn't figure you'd go . . ." Corky said.

Melody thought about it a minute. I should go, she thought. If I stay at the Sniders's I'll just be miserable thinking about Scarlett and Chaz. "On second thought, Corky, I'll go," Melody said.

"For real?" Corky asked. "That would be great! It's the new Winona Ryder movie at the Ten-plex."

"Sounds great," Melody said.

Or at least better than lying in bed crying my eyes out all night, she added in her own mind.

"What I liked about her performance was the honesty of it," Corky was saying, as she and Melody strolled after the movie. "It was like she wasn't sentimental playing the character, you know? She wasn't self-indulgent or anything."

Melody barely remembered anything about the movie; she'd been too miserable—about Chaz dating Scarlett, about how she'd exploded at Scarlett, as if they really were rivals for the same guy, about how totally and utterly she was failing at her mission.

"Are you okay?" Corky asked.

"Sure," Melody said, forcing her mind back to the moment. "You know a lot about acting, don't you?" They were slowly walking toward a nearby restaurant to get something to eat.

Corky shrugged. "I've read a lot of books. And I try to study the plays and movies I see. But Ms. Russell never casts me in the school plays or anything."

"That's totally unfair," Melody said firmly.

"She hates me because I'm fat," Corky said. "Once she asked me in front of a whole room full of kids when I was going to go on a diet."

"That's horrible!" Melody exclaimed.

"It was humiliating," Corky agreed. They walked into the restaurant and found a booth near the window. "I started thumbing through that book you gave me," she said.

"What did you think?" Melody asked.

"Well, the book says that diets don't work," Corky said slowly.

"They don't," Melody said. "There's only so long that you can starve yourself, and then you just gain the weight back. Believe me, I've gained and lost twenty pounds a zillion times."

"Twenty pounds," Corky said wistfully. "That's nothing."

"Well, it was a lot to me," Melody said.

The waiter came over and both girls ordered Chinese chicken salads.

"The thing is, if you eat low-fat, high-carbohydrate foods, you can eat a lot," Melody said. "Oh, and you have to exercise."

"I hate exercising," Corky said, making a face.

"Me too," Melody said.

"But you look gorgeous in a little leotard," Corky said. "There's no way on Earth I'm going to some gym where everyone is gonna laugh at me."

"Exercise at home," Melody said. "That's what I did, because I couldn't afford to join a health club."

When the salads came Melody told Corky more about how she healthfully maintained her weight.

"But I need to lose, like, a hundred pounds or something," Corky said. "You needed to lose twenty!"

"It'll work," Melody insisted. "You just have to stick with it. But think about it—you won't be dieting, and you won't be hungry."

Corky looked at Melody thoughtfully. "Something is missing in all this."

"What?" Melody asked, forking a tomato from her salad.

"You still haven't told me how you got yourself to stop throwing up."

Melody put down her fork. "It was really, really hard," she confessed. "I was . . . well, I guess you could say I was kind of addicted to it. It got to a point where I was purging five times a day, sometimes even more. Then one day I was at a photo shoot, with my head over the toilet . . ."

Melody hesitated a moment. "I remember there was this cockroach crawling up my leg. But all I could think about was that I had to get rid of all the lunch I'd eaten. I was so afraid I wouldn't fit into the clothes I was supposed to model, and then I wouldn't get any work, and then my family would have to go on welfare or something."

She took a deep breath. "So I stuck my finger down my throat. And . . . all this blood started to pour out of my mouth. I was choking to death on my own blood . . ."

"Oh, my God," Corky murmured.

"An ambulance came," Melody reported. "I had ruptured a major blood vessel. They finally got the bleeding under control, but it was the lowest point of my life. And I told myself that I would never, ever be hanging over a toilet again unless I had food poisoning or stomach flu."

"And you never did?" Corky asked.

"I never did," Melody said quietly. "I'm not telling you I'm not still obsessed with my weight, but . . . I'm working on it."

Corky twirled the straw in her diet Coke, then she finally looked up at Melody. "I think I'm going to work on it, too," she said. "I think I'm ready to change."

"I'll help you," Melody promised.

"I'm kind of scared," Corky confessed. "Everyone in my family is fat. If I go on a diet they'll all tease me—"

"But you're not going on a diet," Melody reminded her.

"But what if . . . what if I try and I fail?" Corky asked, tears in her eyes.

"I have a friend named JD," Melody said slowly. "And he once told me that the only failure is not to try at all."

"Yeah, I guess that's true," Corky said, but she sounded scared.

"If you want to do it, do it for yourself," Melody said earnestly. "It can be our secret. And we can exercise together in my room at the Sniders. You help me and I'll help you, okay?"

"Okay," Corky said shyly. "I have to tell you, Melody, you're much cooler than I thought you were. I don't know why you were hanging out with Scarlett Whitmore. She has no soul."

And I haven't exactly helped her get one, either, Melody thought sadly.

"Oh, my God, don't look now—but guess who just walked in?" Corky hissed.

Naturally Melody turned around. And there was Chaz with Scarlett—and she was kissing him.

Nine

Melody tossed and turned over again. She punched her pillow to fluff it into a different position, and she tried to get comfortable for the zillionth time.

It was no use. She couldn't sleep.

She leaned over and looked at the clock on the nightstand. It was three o'clock in the morning.

"This is terrible!" she wailed out loud, turning over on to her back. She stared up at the ceiling, which she could just barely make out by the moonlight streaming in from the window.

She sighed heavily and, like a movie, the scene in the restaurant earlier that night played over again in her mind. Watching Scarlett kissing Chaz. And then the two of them had seen Melody and Corky and they'd come over to their table. Scarlett chatted with Melody about this and that, pointedly ignoring Corky. And as she talked, she clung to Chaz like moss on a tree.

Melody had tried to not even make eye contact with Chaz, because she knew looking at him would be too painful. But finally, when she didn't think she could stand it another instant, she'd looked up, hoping to see some glimmer of caring for her in his eyes.

But Chaz had been looking at Scarlett.

It was one of the worst moments of Melody's life—or death.

Finally, Chaz and Scarlett had gone to their own booth. Melody had gone pale, and Corky asked her about it, but there was no way Melody could explain. She just paid her part of the check and went home as soon as she possibly could.

And now here it was, hours later, and she was still awake, still replaying that horrible scene in her mind.

"JD, how could you do this to me?" Melody wailed. "Why did you have to make this so hard?"

Ping.

What was that?

There had been some kind of noise at the window. Or had it been Melody's imagination?

Ping.

There *was* noise at the window. But what could it be? Melody's room was on the second floor.

Maybe it's JD, Melody thought hopefully, getting out of bed. Although I don't know why he'd make noise at the window when he could just make himself appear in my room.

She padded over to the window just as something hit it hard. *Thwack.*

This time the noise was much louder than before. A large stone had hit the glass, creating a razor line crack down the center.

Melody raised the window and peered down into the backyard.

And there, illuminated by the moonlight, was Chaz, who had been throwing increasingly larger stones at her window.

Chaz!

"What are you doing?" she whispered loudly.

"Throwing stones at your window!" Chaz whispered back.

"Why don't you go throw stones at Scarlett's window?" Melody asked. Then she clapped her hand to her mouth. "I can't believe I said that," she added quickly.

"Come down," Chaz begged.

"All I have on is a T-shirt," she said.

"So?" he asked. "Please, come down."

Melody quickly shut the window, then she tiptoed down the hall and ran quickly down the stairs and outside into the backyard.

"Hi," Chaz said shyly. He had on jeans, a sweatshirt, and a denim jacket, and Melody thought she had never seen anyone look more handsome.

"Hi," Melody replied. She shivered in the night air. All she was wearing was a long white T-shirt. Chaz took off his jacket and put it around her shoulders.

"I couldn't sleep," he told her. "I'm sorry if I woke you up . . ."

"I couldn't sleep, either," she admitted.

"I was just laying there, feeling miserable," Chaz went on. "And then I remembered something this friend of mine named Kurt told me had happened with his girlfriend. They had had a fight, and he felt really awful. And he couldn't sleep. So he went over to her house in the middle of the night and threw stones at her window to wake her up. I figured it was worth a shot. Of course, I didn't figure I'd actually crack the glass . . ."

Melody smiled a little. "I'll explain it somehow, and I'll pay the Sniders to have it fixed—"

"No, I'll pay," Chaz insisted.

"It's okay—"

"No, really—"

They stopped and stared at each other, then they both broke up laughing.

"This is really dumb, huh?" Chaz finally said.

"It is," Melody agreed. "Especially since all the money we have comes from JD, anyway."

Chaz reached out and took Melody's hand. "I just had to come talk to you. When I saw you tonight at the restaurant, that was so hard . . ."

"But you wouldn't even look at me!" Melody protested. "You just kept staring at Scarlett!"

"I was afraid to look at you," Chaz admitted. "I was so sure that the truth would, like, jump right out at everyone."

"What truth?" Melody asked shyly.

"That I don't care about Scarlett Whitmore at all," he said. "That the only girl I want to be with is you."

"Really?" Melody asked in a small voice.

"I don't know why JD decided I had to come down here to date Scarlett," Chaz said earnestly. "I guess that's part of the whole gig up there—that we don't get to understand everything, but we have to learn from it, anyway . . ." He hesitated for a moment. "But . . . I've never felt about anyone the way I feel about you," he finally said in a low voice. "And this mission is just about the hardest thing I ever had to do."

"Me, too," Melody agreed, a lump in her throat.

"I know I told you I wanted to wait to kiss you," Chaz went on, "so you'd know how really special you are to me . . ."

"Yes?" Melody whispered.

"Well, do you know it yet?" Chaz asked.

"Yes," Melody replied, her heart pounding in her chest.

He gazed deeply into Melody's eyes, and she could see how sincere he really was. Then he gently took her in his arms and gently kissed her.

Melody wrapped her arms around him. The kiss began softly, sweetly, then their passion for each other fueled it until they were totally lost in each other's arms.

And then it happened.

The world spun away.

Suddenly Chaz and Melody found themselves amidst the stars, flying through the air.

"Oh, my God, what happened?" Melody cried, terribly frightened. The wind rushed through her hair and she clung to Chaz, scared to death. "Did we do something awful?"

"I don't know!" Chaz said, holding tight to Melody. "JD!" he called out. "Help us!"

Then, just like that, they landed back in the Sniders' backyard, exactly where they had been before.

"What was that?" Melody asked, shaking so hard she could barely get the words out.

"Whoa," was all Chaz could utter.

They both looked up at the stars, awestruck.

"Do you think JD is mad at us?" Melody asked, turning to Chaz.

"Hey, JD!" Chaz called. "Are you ticked off?"

JD appeared suddenly, leaning against a nearby tree. "Some kiss," he said appreciatively.

"Did we do something wrong?" Melody asked anxiously.

"What do you think?" JD asked.

"Well, I suppose our being together isn't exactly our mission," she said slowly.

"True," JD agreed.

"But you can't expect us to both be down here and pretend we don't have feelings for each other," Chaz argued.

"Also true," JD agreed.

Chaz shook his head with annoyance. "Ya know, JD, sometimes you really drive me crazy."

"Yeah, I can be maddening, can't I?" JD agreed with a grin. "Anyway, buckaroos, not to worry about the little cosmic jaunt you just took. What happens is that sometimes when two Teen Angels kiss on Earth with that much—uh—shall we say feeling?—something happens in the cosmos. Very rock 'n' roll, don't ya think?"

"So we didn't mess up?" Melody asked.

"That, babe, is part of what you need to figure out," JD said.

"You always say that—" Chaz began.

"And I'm always right," JD added. "You guys are doing good. Just keep in mind the reason why you're down here. And remember that knowledge is power. Got that?"

"But what are we supposed to—" Melody began.

"Listen, babe, hate to interrupt, but I gotta fly," JD said. "Catch ya on the rebound!" And he was gone.

Chaz folded his arms. "For someone whose favorite expression is 'never hurry, never worry,' he sure does hurry a lot, doesn't he?"

"What does that mean, 'knowledge is power'?" Melody asked, her brow furrowed.

Chaz put his arms around her. "Right now, Mel,

with all due respect to JD, I don't feel like thinking about it." He gently brought her face to his, but right before they kissed, they both pulled back.

"Are you thinking what I'm thinking?" Chaz asked.

Melody looked up at the stars. "There isn't any chance we could actually get *lost* up there, is there?"

"That," Chaz murmured, pulling Melody closer, "is a chance I'm willing to take."

"Hi, Mel," Scarlett said, coming up next to her in the hall the next morning.

"Oh, hi," Melody said. She turned the combination on her locker and reached in to get out two textbooks. Even though she'd gotten barely two hours of sleep, she felt fabulous.

"So, don't you want to hear about my date last night?" Scarlett asked, leaning against the locker next to Melody's.

"Not really," Melody said. Then she remembered the vow she'd made to herself right around dawn, when Chaz had finally left the Sniders's house. She had to perform better in her mission. Now that she felt secure that Chaz really didn't care about Scarlett, and he really did care about her, she needed to keep her mind focused on her reason for being at Ground Zero.

"I mean," Melody amended, "I saw the two of you together, remember? I could tell it was going really well."

"What were you doing with Porky McGee, anyway?" Scarlett asked.

"Please stop calling her that," Melody said. "I like her. She's my friend."

"Well, I guess there's no accounting for taste,"

Scarlett said. She flicked the hair off her face. "Chaz is crazed for me," she confided.

"Really?" Melody asked carefully.

"He was all over me last night," Scarlett said. "Tell me everything you know about him."

"I don't know him that well," Melody said, closing her locker. They walked slowly toward their English classroom.

"Does he have a girlfriend back in Detroit?" Scarlett asked.

"I'm not sure," Melody hedged.

"Not that I couldn't get him away from her, because I could," Scarlett said with bravado. They turned the corner. "Don't you think I could?"

"I wouldn't know," Melody said politely. She badly wanted to change the subject. "So, which public service did you sign up to do this afternoon?"

"I didn't," Scarlett said.

"But you have to do one," Melody reminded her. "And today is the first day. I signed up to go work in a soup kitchen downtown. Want to come with me?"

"No," Scarlett said. "But I suppose the soup kitchen is as good a choice as any."

"Maybe it'll be fun," Melody said. "We can go in my car. I'll meet you in the parking lot at one o'clock, okay?"

"Whatever," Scarlett said, as they walked into their English class. "At least we get out of school for a little while."

"Hi," Chaz said casually to Melody and Scarlett, as he walked into the classroom. He stopped at Scarlett's desk. "I had fun last night."

"I know you did," Scarlett said coolly, a small grin on her lips.

Chaz laughed. "You're not nearly as tough as you pretend to be, Scarlett." Then he walked to his seat in the back of the room.

Scarlett leaned over to Melody. "I'm going to make sure Jeff sees me with Chaz today. He'll be livid."

Melody sighed. It was all just so stupid and tiresome. But she must do it because she feels insecure, Melody thought. That's got to be it. I think.

"Chaz has feelings you know," Melody said.

"Duh," Scarlett uttered.

"Who is it you want, Scarlett?" Melody asked. "Is it Jeff or is it Chaz?"

"I want Jeff to pay for . . . you know," Scarlett said, quickly looking around to make sure no one had overheard her.

"And Chaz?"

"I like him," Scarlett admitted. "I really, really like him. More than I've ever liked anyone, maybe."

It sounded to Melody that Scarlett was actually being sincere. She knew she should feel happy, but once again she found herself feeling threatened and jealous.

"Hi, Scarlett!" Jennifer said, taking her seat. "So, how was Chaz? Tell me everything!"

Scarlett and Jennifer whispered together until Dr. Capelli began the class.

All day long Melody tried not to think about how Scarlett really liked Chaz, and about Scarlett's comment that Chaz had been 'all over her' the night before.

It isn't true, she told herself. She'd just bragging because she feels insecure that Jeff dumped her. Chaz would never do that.

Would he?

What if he has to do it as part of his mission? Melody worried.

No. JD would never do that to me.

Would he?

Around and around Melody's mind went, until she thought she would go totally crazy.

By the time she met Scarlett to leave for the soup kitchen, she was exhausted and anxious. She hadn't been able to spend any time alone with Chaz during the day. It was almost as if what had happened between them the night before was some kind of dream.

"I'm going out with Chaz again tonight," Scarlett confided to Melody as they pulled out of the school's parking lot.

"What about play rehearsal?" Melody asked. Her fingers unconsciously grasped the steering wheel so hard that her knuckles turned white.

"After," Scarlett said. "A late date. Pretty romantic, huh?"

"Won't your parents mind?" Melody asked, her eyes on the road.

"Please," Scarlett snorted. "My mother is—well, you know how my mother is. And Daddy dearest is too busy playing with his secretary to know if I'm even alive."

That is so terrible for you, Melody wanted to say. But she knew it wouldn't get her anywhere. So she decided to try a totally different tact. "Lucky you, huh?" she said, stopping at a red light.

"How do you mean?" Scarlett asked, as she pulled her brush out of her purse and began brushing her honey-colored hair.

"No one to check up on you," Melody said. "You can do whatever you want whenever you want."

"Yeah, it's great," Scarlett said.

"And it's really lucky that your mom rags on you so much about your looks, too," Melody said. "That way you'll never let yourself go."

"Right," Scarlett said, staring at Melody.

"So I guess your life is just about perfect," Melody continued in her soft voice.

"Uh-huh," Scarlett said. Melody waited for her to say more, but for the rest of the trip she just stared out the window and ignored Melody.

"This is it," Melody said, pulling into a metered parking spot in front of the soup kitchen. It was an old brick building on a side street downtown. Four or five men were hanging out in front, talking and smoking cigarettes. Their clothes looked shabby and worn.

"Oh look, there's Corky." The heavy girl was just pulling her car into a parking spot across the street. "I didn't know she was doing this community service."

"Gee, you're such great buds, how could you have missed it?" Scarlett said sarcastically.

"Corky happens to be smart, talented, and interesting," Melody said, surprised at the firmness of her own voice. *I'm really starting to stand up for myself!* she realized happily. *I really am!*

"She's also an oinker," Scarlett added as they got out of the car.

"Well, I guess that's something else you don't have to worry about," Melody said, trying for a light tone. "Lucky you—again."

"Hi," Corky said, after she had crossed the street toward them. "How's it going?"

"You would volunteer for the soup kitchen," Scarlett said nastily. "Free food."

"And you would make some bitchy comment," Corky said defiantly. She took a deep breath. "I really wonder, Scarlett. What's it like to be as cruel as you are? I mean, you must really hate yourself to be so awful to me."

Scarlett's jaw dropped. Then her face turned bright red. She looked from Melody, to Corky, and back at Melody. "Listen," she spat out. "I want you to know your pathetic attempt at reverse psychology in the car was a joke." Then she turned on Corky. "And as for you, at least when I look at myself in the mirror, a disgusting slob isn't looking back at me."

"I can always lose weight, Scarlett," Corky said in a level voice, "but unfortunately it seems like you will always be ugly."

Then Corky turned on her heels and walked away.

Well, I'll be, Melody thought with admiration. Corky really and truly stuck up for herself. I guess she's not going to be Scarlett's silent victim anymore. Maybe Corky and I are both changing!

"That big fat—" Scarlett began.

"She's right, though," Melody said.

"Is that what you think?" Scarlett asked. "I thought we were supposed to be friends! Not that I care—"

"But you do care," Melody said earnestly. "Look, I'm sorry if my—what did you call it?—reverse psychology was stupid. I guess I'm not all that clever. But I know that you're hurting inside, Scarlett, and you just refuse to admit it—"

"Who says I'm hurting?" Scarlett exclaimed. "That is so stupid—"

"I saw how much your mom hurt you," Melody said. "And I know how much it hurt when Jeff dropped you. I saw how you are with Pickles, how much you care because she's wounded like you are—''

"Oh, you think you have it all figured out, is that it?" Scarlett said hotly.

"No, not all," Melody said. "But some of it, maybe. You don't have to be so tough and cool and mean all the time. You really don't. I know that deep down that's not who you really are."

Scarlett's lower lip trembled for a moment. This is it! Melody thought with excitement. I'm finally getting through to her.

But then just as quickly as it began, it stopped. Scarlett's chin jutted into the air. "For your information," she finally said, "I happen to be perfectly happy. Your problem is that you're jealous because Chaz wants me and not you. Do you think I haven't seen how you look at him when you think no one else is looking?"

Melody couldn't say anything. How could she deny her feelings for Chaz?

"I knew I was right!" Scarlett exclaimed triumphantly. "You probably don't even have a boyfriend back in Detroit! It's always been Chaz you want! That's why you acted so weird when he showed up at Whitmore! I have it all figured out now!"

"No, you don't—" Melody began.

"Really?" Scarlett said coolly. She knew she had the upperhand. "Explain it to me, then."

Melody just stood there. What could she say?

"I *knew* it!" Scarlett crowed. "Well, too bad, Melody. Tonight I plan to make him all mine. And I do mean *all*."

Ten

Melody stared at her face in the dressing room mirror. "Tonight you're going on stage in a play," she told herself. "And everyone is going to find out that your mother was right—you don't have any talent."

It was finally opening night for *Bus Stop*. Melody was in the empty dressing room she would be sharing with Scarlett, putting the finishing touches on her makeup. The curtain for the show was scheduled to go up in an hour, and already people were milling around outside the theater, waiting for the house to open so that they could get good seats, which were available first come, first serve.

As she stared at her own reflection, Melody thought back on everything that had happened in the past few days. Ever since she and Scarlett had had that fight outside of the soup kitchen, Scarlett had refused to speak to her. Chaz had come over to the Sniders's house twice, very late at night, but they'd both agreed that they had to cool their relationship while they were at Ground Zero, for the good of the mission.

I know it was the mature thing to do, Melody thought to herself, but that doesn't mean I like it.

They had agreed to discuss Scarlett only insofar as the mission was concerned, which meant that Melody couldn't even ask Chaz if Scarlett had made good on her promise to "make Chaz all mine."

Melody had kept herself as busy as she possibly could so that she wouldn't have to think about all the problems in her life. She and Corky had exercised together four times already. She'd caught up on all her homework for Whitmore High and Teen Heaven High (Corky had helped a lot with the tougher subjects), and she'd spent endless hours working on the play.

But still, it wasn't enough.

At night she lay in bed, staring at the ceiling, imagining Scarlett and Chaz together. Everyone at Whitmore High knew they were a couple. And every time Melody saw them together, it was like a knife in her heart. Everyone also assumed they'd gone all the way, probably because Scarlett hinted all the time that they had.

But he just couldn't have, Melody thought, gripping the edge of the makeup table. JD would never want him to do that! So why do I feel so totally, terribly insecure?

Melody sighed and picked up the blush brush. Between worrying about her role in the play, about failing at her mission, and about Chaz and Scarlett, she felt like a total wreck.

"Nervous?" Corky said to Melody, sticking her head into the dressing room.

"I'm petrified," Melody admitted, as she shakily tried to apply some blush to her cheeks.

"Let me help you," said Corky, who was dressed in an all-black outfit. She sat down on a stool next to Melody.

Melody nodded, and Corky took the blush brush and applied makeup quickly and efficiently to Melody's face.

"You look like you've done that before," Melody said, admiring Corky's work in the mirror.

"When you don't get cast," Corky said diffidently, "you end up putting makeup on a lot of faces."

"Maybe that'll change soon," Melody said softly.

"Not unless Ms. Russell gets fired," Corky pointed out. She put the blush brush down. "I wanted to tell you, when I put my jeans on this morning, they felt looser."

"That's terrific!" Melody said.

"Yeah," Corky agreed, but she looked troubled.

"What is it?"

"I don't know, it's hard to explain . . ." She pushed some hair behind her ear and got up from the stool. "I want to lose weight, but on the other hand, it makes me so angry that people won't accept me as I am. Do you know what I mean?"

Melody nodded. "I know exactly what you mean."

"Sometimes I have these fantasies . . . like, I get really thin and cute, and then some guy who called me 'Porky' when I was fat falls madly in love with me, and I don't give him the time of day. In fact, I get great joy out of breaking his heart."

"Because those guys hurt you, Corky," Melody said. "They really wounded you. I can understand your wanting revenge."

"Yeah," Corky mumbled. She stared out the window a moment. "The world is based on such superficial stuff sometimes, huh?"

"This world, maybe," Melody said.

"What do you mean?"

"Oh, nothing," Melody said. "Ignore me. Hey, do I need more powder?"

Corky walked toward Melody and scrutinized her face. "Yeah, you'll shine under the lights halfway into act one unless you lay it on."

"Thanks," Melody said with a smile.

"No prob," Corky said. She stood there awkwardly a second. "You're great, Melody," she finally said. "Really."

"So are you," Melody said quietly.

"Yeah, I am," Corky agreed. "But you're the first one at this school who figured it out." She smiled at Melody, then said, "So, break a leg."

"Thanks," Melody said gratefully. "Any great ideas on how to be less nervous?"

"Nope," Corky said honestly. "Just try to use it, I guess."

"I feel like throwing up," Melody admitted.

"Then do it," Corky said, a thin smile crossing her lips. "Just don't do it every day."

Right then a knock came at the dressing room door.

"I'll get it," Corky said, motioning for Melody to stay in her seat. She went over and opened the door.

"Flower delivery," a middle-aged man said to her, thrusting a bouquet of red roses at Corky.

"Thanks," Corky replied, taking the flowers. She looked at the little card that had been thrust into the middle of the roses. "Melody, they're for you."

"For me?" Melody responded, genuinely surprised. Oh, they must be from Chaz! she realized. That was so sweet of him! He really does care about me!

Melody put the flowers down and eagerly opened the little card that was attached. She read:

Melody—

*Harpeth Hall is rooting for you. Break a leg!
We'll be here to cheer.*

—Sarah and Sara and Sayrah

They weren't from Chaz at all. Melody tried hard not to be disappointed.

"So, who are they from?" Corky asked.

"These three really nice girls from Harpeth Hall," Melody said. "I only met them once, but they told me they always come to see the Whitmore school plays. Wasn't that sweet?"

Another knock sounded at the door. Corky looked at her watch before she went to answer it.

"Flower delivery," a young man said, thrusting a vase with a dozen long-stemmed red roses at Corky.

"If I stay in here I'm never going to get anything done," Corky said. She looked at the name on the envelope nestled inbetween the flowers. "They're for Scarlett."

"Did I hear my name?" Scarlett asked as she sailed into the dressing room.

"The flowers are for you," Corky reported. "See you later, Melody." She then walked out the door.

Scarlett quickly opened the little card attached to her roses. "Beautiful roses for a beautiful girl," Scarlett read out loud. "All my love, Chaz."

Melody felt sick to her stomach, but she knew she had to hide it. "That's nice," she managed weakly.

"Yes, he's crazed for me," Scarlett said. She set her purse down and put an elastic band over her hair to hold it away from her face. "I told you I was going to make him all mine, Melody, and I did."

All my love, Chaz. It played over and over in Melody's mind.

"It's none of my business," she finally mumbled, moving the makeup around on her dressing table with trembling fingers.

"No need to be a sore loser," Scarlett said, as she spread makeup base over her face.

"I'm not any kind of a loser," Melody said, trying to steady her voice. "I'm glad you're happy. Maybe caring about Chaz will make you into a nicer person."

"Oh, damn, I left my new false eyelashes with my mother," Scarlett said, totally ignoring Melody's remark. "It's a good thing they don't serve wine at high school plays. Maybe there's a chance she's still sober." She hurried out of the room.

Melody took a deep breath. I have to concentrate on the play, she told herself. I can't think about Scarlett and Chaz right now. What is my first line? Oh, no, I can't even remember my first line . . .

"Can I come in?"

Standing in the doorway, looking as sweet as ever, was Chaz Denton.

"I came to wish you good luck," Chaz said. "Can I come in?"

"Okay," Melody said quietly.

"So . . . are you nervous?"

Melody nodded. She looked over at the flowers Chaz had sent to Scarlett. "Nice flowers."

Chaz looked at Melody closely. "I hurt your feelings," he realized.

"No—"

"Yes," Chaz said. "I'm supposed to be her boyfriend, Melody, I had to send her flowers—"

"It's okay," Melody said. "I understand."

You could have sent me some, too, she thought to herself, gulping hard.

Chaz raked his fingers through his hair. "I think this whole mission sucks, Mel," he said. He looked up at the ceiling. "I'm sorry, JD, but that's what I think."

"Why do you think that?" Melody asked.

"Because I don't feel like either one of us is getting anywhere with Scarlett," Chaz said. "And because you and I are both miserable."

"You, too?" Melody asked.

"What, you think I like pretending to be interested in Scarlett? Do you think I like not being able to be with you? I hate it!"

"You do?" Melody asked in a small voice.

"Yeah, don't you know that by now?" Chaz asked earnestly.

Melody looked over at the roses Chaz had sent to Scarlett again. "I know this is small of me," she said, "but did you really have to sign the card 'all my love'?"

"What?" Chaz asked.

"Your card to Scarlett," Melody said, cocking her head toward the flowers.

"I didn't sign it 'all my love,' " Chaz said.

"But Scarlett read it to me!" Melody exclaimed.

Chaz strode across the dressing room and picked up the card. Then he handed it to Melody.

" 'Beautiful flowers for a beautiful girl,' " Melody read. " 'Chaz.' " She looked up at him, her eyes shining. "She lied to me!"

"Evidently," Chaz said. "I would never say those words unless I meant them, Melody, which means I couldn't say them to Scarlett." He reached into his back pocket and brought out a small jewelry box, which he handed to Melody. "This is for you."

She opened it slowly. Inside was a tiny gold angel pin, just like the one Cisco had given to Shayne Stone when she'd fallen in love with him on her mission.

"Oh, Chaz—" Melody said breathily.

"I thought you could wear it somewhere on your costume," Chaz said. "It's so small I don't think anyone will see it or anything. I didn't want to give you flowers, because they die. I wanted to give you something that would last."

Tears welled in Melody's eyes as she pinned the tiny angel on the collar. "I love it so much!"

"Not as much as I love you," Chaz said in a low voice.

Had he really said it? Had she imagined it? Melody looked up at Chaz, and shining in his eyes she saw all the love for her that she felt for him.

The next thing she knew she was in his arms, and he was kissing her passionately.

"I love you so much!" she whispered. "I was so scared—"

"Never again," Chaz said in a husky voice. "You'll never have to be scared again . . ."

They lost themselves in each other again, locked in a passionate embrace.

"And this is my dressing room," Melody dimly heard. "I have to share it with—oh, my God!"

It was Scarlett, standing in the doorway. With her mother.

Melody and Chaz jumped apart, but not soon enough.

"You witch!" Scarlett screamed, her face going completely white.

"Scarlett, I'm sorry, I—" Melody began.

"I hate you both!" Scarlett hissed, tears in her eyes. "I'll hate you forever! Forever!" She turned and ran away before Chaz could even open his mouth.

Mrs. Whitmore stared at Chaz with a look of sadness in her eyes. "Hasn't she been hurt enough?" she asked. Then she slowly walked away.

"I can't believe we let that happen," Chaz said in a shaky voice. He sat down in the nearest chair and put his head in his hands.

"We should go after her!" Melody cried.

"And say what?" Chaz asked. "How can we possibly explain?"

"We can't," Melody realized. She sat down heavily. "How could we do it? I've ruined everything! All I was thinking about was myself . . ."

"We're in this together, Mel," Chaz said. "I shouldn't have even come to the dressing room. I should have waited to tell you until the mission was over . . ."

Silence. Neither of them knew what to say.

From outside the dressing room they heard nervous voices and frantic activity.

"Half hour," Corky called, sticking her head into the dressing room.

"Corky, we have a big problem," Melody said before the stage manager could leave.

"What?"

Melody looked over at Chaz.

"Scarlett caught me kissing Melody," Chaz explained. "Her mother saw it, too. She ran out of here. I don't know where she went."

"Or when she'll come back," Melody added.

Corky looked from Melody to Chaz, and back at Melody. "Wow," she finally said. "You mean Scarlett Whitmore got a taste of her own medicine?"

"I shouldn't have done it," Melody moaned.

"She'll come back in time for the play," Chaz said. "Won't she?"

"I'd better tell Ms. Russell," Corky decided. "Just in case."

Melody stood up. "I feel like I should go look for her—"

"You'd better not," Corky said. "I have a feeling seeing you would only make things worse. I mean, she hates me, but she didn't catch me kissing her boyfriend." Corky quickly left the dressing room, shutting the door behind her.

Melody turned to Chaz. "JD is never going to forgive us for this."

"Maybe he will," Chaz said, but he didn't sound at all certain.

"What do you think the Big Guy does when a Teen Angel messes up this much?" Melody asked in a small voice.

"Look, it was my fault," Chaz said. "I'll explain it to JD—"

"I'm so mad at myself!" Melody cried. "I got so wrapped up in my own problems that I didn't think about Scarlett at all!" Her face paled. "Chaz, you don't think JD'll send us to . . ."

"Deep Six?" Chaz put in. "No. I'm sure he won't."

They both sat there, not knowing what to do.

"I'm so sorry," Melody whispered, looking up at the ceiling.

"Me, too," Chaz added, also looking at the ceiling. "JD? JD? Can you hear us?"

There was a knock at the door.

"JD!" Chaz cried, running to open it.

It was Ms. Russell.

"What happened to Scarlett?" she demanded in a high voice.

"She . . . she got upset," Melody said, biting her lower lip.

"Well, Mrs. Whitmore just told me that Scarlett went home with the stomach flu, and she isn't coming back! She's not going on in the play!"

Eleven

"But she can't do that!" Corky protested. "How can she just walk out on everyone?"

"It appears that she did," Ms. Russell said. She clapped her hand to her forehead. "My show is ruined!"

Melody thought quickly. She turned to Corky. "You should go on."

"*What*?" Ms. Russell practically screamed.

"Corky knows the lines," Melody said. "I know she does. Don't you?"

"Well, yes, but—" Corky began.

"You should go on as Cherie," Melody maintained. "You could carry the script with you if you want to, but I know you know the part. You've been at every single rehearsal—"

"I can't do it!" Corky protested.

"Why not?" Melody asked.

"It's absurd!" Ms. Russell yelled. "We'll just have to cancel the performance." She put her hand to her forehead again. "This has never happened to me before, not in twenty years of teaching drama . . ."

"It doesn't have to happen to you now," Chaz said. "Let Corky go on."

Ms. Russell took a deep breath. "Look, it is not my intention to be cruel. I am only saying what I'm about to say to spare you embarrassment, Corky. You couldn't possibly fit into Scarlett's costumes. Plus, the audience would laugh at you."

Corky blushed a bright red, and her head seemed to sag into her chest. "I guess that's true . . ."

"I'll just have to go out there and tell everyone . . . something," Ms. Russell said.

"Wait!" Melody cried. "Okay, it's true. People might expect the character of Cherie to be thin. And some of the idiots at this school might laugh at you, Corky. But only at first." Melody walked over to Corky and forced the other girl to look her in the eye. "Only at first," she said again. "Don't you see? Your talent will win them over. I know it will. This is the chance for everyone in the school to see how talented you really are. I know you can do it."

"But . . . but the costumes," Corky stammered.

"The costumes don't matter," Chaz said. He stood up and walked over to Corky, too. "Nothing matters but how well you can play the part. I know you can do it, too."

"So I should just . . . go on in my own clothes?" Corky asked in a quivering voice.

"Right," Melody said.

"And carry the script?"

"Right," Chaz agreed.

"And you guys really, really think I can do it?" Corky asked, her eyes pleading with them.

"We know you can," Melody told her.

"I haven't agreed to this!" Ms. Russell cried.

Melody turned to her. "You really don't have a choice, Ms. Russell," she said. "You can't disappoint the entire school and cancel the play when there's an alternative, can you?"

Ms. Russell stood there a moment, her glasses slipping down her nose. She pushed them back up. "All right," she finally said. Then she turned on her heels and left.

Melody hugged a shocked Corky. "Let's get you ready!" she cried. "You are about to become a star!"

Melody took a bow with the rest of the cast, the applause washing over her.

Then Corky came out, all by herself, for the final bow. And as one the entire audience stood up, yelling, "Bravo!" and clapping as hard as they possibly could.

Corky had been brilliant. Yes, at first some kids had been rude enough to laugh. Some even yelled things out, which threw off Corky for a while. But the longer she was on stage the more she became the lonely, insecure Cherie, who so badly needed someone to truly love her. Finally the audience forgot that Corky was overweight or that she wasn't wearing a costume—they simply got lost in the world of the play.

Corky joined the cast in a group bow. Then Chaz brought out the roses from Scarlett's dressing room, and he presented them to Corky, who was crying like a baby.

When everyone ran off stage, Melody hugged Corky as hard as she could. "You were wonderful! You were so wonderful!"

"I can't believe I did it!" Corky cried, tears of happiness streaming down her cheeks.

"Corky, you were great!" a girl from the stage crew called over to them.

"You're really talented!" another boy added as he walked by.

"Thanks!" Corky said, her eyes shining.

"Well, Corky," Ms. Russell said, walking over to them. "You were good."

"Good!" Chaz protested. "She was fantastic!"

"She wasn't right for the part," Ms. Russell maintained before she walked away.

"Just ignore her," Melody advised.

"She was right, actually," Corky said. "I wasn't right for the part. But now I know I can do it, and nothing she can say or do is going to stop me!"

"Hey, Corky, you were terrific, no lie!" Gray Morse said, walking over to them. Jeff Walker was with him.

"Thanks, Greg," Corky said.

"Scarlett got sick, huh?" Jeff asked.

"I heard she isn't really sick," Scarlett's friend, Jennifer said, overhearing them. "I heard she just walked out for some reason!"

"That sounds like Scarlett," Jeff said. "She's a spoiled brat. Anyway, Corky, that was the best performance I ever saw at this school. You should think about becoming a professional actress."

"Thanks, Jeff," Corky said, holding tightly to her flowers. "I will."

"Corky! Corky!" a girl yelled from across the stage. "Come over here! I want to get a photo of you!"

"Excuse me," Corky said, and she hurried off.

"I'm so proud of her," Melody said, smiling after her friend.

"I'm so proud of *you*," Chaz said.

"Me?" Melody questioned. "But I messed up in a major way!"

"You were wonderful to Corky," Chaz said. "And you were wonderful in the play. You're really talented, Melody."

Melody thought for a moment. "Do you think maybe JD gave me acting talent for the time I'm down here, like he arranged for me to be able to do gymnastics for the cheerleading squad?"

"No," Chaz said. "I think it was all you."

"It's funny," Melody said softly. "I was so busy thinking about Corky that I forgot to be scared! And then once the play started, I just . . . just lost myself in the part!"

"Well, you were great," Chaz said with a smile. "Your mom was wrong, you know. You really do have acting talent."

"Oh, no, I don't think so—"

"I do," Chaz said. "I definitely do." He put his arms around her and gave her a light kiss.

"We shouldn't—" Melody said quickly.

"I think we've already ruined our little charade," Chaz said dryly. "Whatever happens, happens. You with me?"

"I'm with you," Melody agreed, and she gave herself up to a wonderful kiss.

"A-hem," Melody heard, as someone ostentatiously cleared their throat behind her.

She turned around.

It was JD, leaning against a piece of the set.

"JD!" Melody cried.

"Nice show," JD said easily.

"You were out there?" Chaz asked.

"I caught the second act," JD said. "You were

136

really good, babe. And your friend, Corky, is a major talent. Too bad about Scarlett.''

Melody and Chaz exchanged a guilty look.

"Look, JD, it was my fault—" Chaz began.

"No, it was my fault," Melody insisted. "Don't blame him. It was my mission and I failed."

"I should never have gone to her dressing room," Chaz said. "I knew it was too much temptation—"

"I thought about myself more than I thought about Scarlett—" Melody said.

"Hold up, hold up," JD said, holding his palms up to them. "Let's not start whipping ourselves yet, okay?"

"Hey, Melody! You were so good!" Beth said, quickly walking over to them. She saw JD. "Well, hi," she added flirtatiously. "And who are you?"

"He's my . . . cousin," Melody invented.

"Do you live around here?" Beth asked.

"Pretty far from here, actually," JD said.

"Too bad," Beth purred. "So, will you be visiting Melody for a while? Maybe I could show you around Nashville."

"Gee, it's a short trip," JD said, regret filling his voice. "Maybe next time."

"Okay," Beth agreed. She contemplated JD for a minute. "You know, you remind me of someone. Someone in the movies . . ."

"Brad Pitt?" JD asked.

"No," Beth said. "I can't put my finger on it. Well, it was nice to meet you, cuz." She walked away.

"*Brad Pitt*?" Chaz asked JD.

"I try to keep up," JD said with a shrug. "What say we take this conversation elsewhere, gang." He snapped his fingers, and the next instant Melody and Chaz found themselves with JD in the Center of Everything back in Teen Heaven.

"You mean it's all over?" Melody asked in shock.

"Not quite," JD said. "But this seemed like a good place for us to chat. Don't worry. When you go back down you'll only have been missing for, like, a split second."

"So we are going back down, then?" Chaz asked. "Listen, JD, about Scarlett. Melody really tried. I know she did. If you send her back down until she gets Scarlett to change, she could end up being at Ground Zero forever!"

"Yeah, Scarlett is a tough one," JD agreed, scratching his chin. "It didn't work out too well."

"I failed," Melody said in a small voice. "I'm so sorry, JD. I tried. But I didn't know how to get through to her—"

"Live, die, and learn, I always say," JD said with a shrug.

"I just feel like such a total failure," Melody said, her eyes filling with tears. "Cisco and Nicole did such wonderful jobs on their first mission, and I . . . well, I flunked."

"Yo, Mel, please, stop beating yourself up!" JD said.

"I just feel so terrible!" Melody cried.

"Hey, remember how I told you that knowledge is power?" JD asked patiently.

"Right," Melody agreed.

"So, what did you learn?" JD asked.

Melody thought a minute. "Well, I learned to be more assertive—I hope. And I learned why Scarlett is so unhappy. And I learned that just because I wanted her to change didn't mean she was ready to change.''

JD nodded. ''Right. There's this little thing called free will. Maybe you heard about it.''

''Meaning that Scarlett had to want to change?'' Chaz asked.

''Something like that,'' JD agreed. ''I mean, you guys are angels, you know? You're not the Big Guy. You can't make things go how you want them to. And you can't *make* people change.''

''But I feel like I could have done a better job,'' Melody said with a frown.

''Me, too,'' Chaz agreed.

''Yeah, well, that's a horse of a different color, as we say,'' JD said. ''So, how could you have done better?''

''I let my personal relationship with Chaz get in the way of my mission,'' Melody admitted in a low voice.

''Ditto,'' Chaz echoed.

''Yeah, I think so, too,'' JD said. ''I guess we're gonna have to send the two of you to Deep Six—''

''Oh, no!'' Melody cried. ''Please! We'll do better—''

''Yo, Mel, chill!'' JD interrupted. ''I was only kidding!''

''You were?'' Chaz asked, as shaken as Melody.

''Of course!'' JD said. ''You think the Big Guy would axe you just because you aren't perfect? I mean, give Him a little credit!''

''So He isn't mad at us?'' Melody asked in a low voice.

''Not mad, not glad, just watching,'' JD said. ''Frankly, He and I had a little chat. I personally think He was very hard on you for your first mission, Melody.''

"You disagreed with the Big Guy?" Chaz asked in awe.

"Not a problem," JD said airily. "You think He doesn't ever make a mistake?"

"The Big Guy makes mistakes?" Melody asked in shock.

"Let's just say I don't always agree with him," JD said with a shrug. "Hey, it's tough bein' the Ultimate, you know what I'm saying? Besides, something really, really cool happened while you were Down Below, if you recall."

"What?" Melody asked, confused.

"A friend you made named Corky?" JD asked. "Ring any bells?"

"I wish she had been my mission," Melody said with a sigh.

"Look at it this way," JD said. "Scarlett was your mission, but she didn't want to change. Corky wasn't your mission, but she did want to change. And it had everything to do with you coming into her life. That free will thing is a real kicker, ya know? You did good, kid."

"I did?" Melody asked in a daze. "But I wasn't trying to, we just got to be friends . . ."

"Funny how it all works out sometimes," JD said with a chuckle. "So, here's the scoop. The Angel Point situation on this gig might not be all you hoped for, guys. I mean, we're all in agreement that you could have done better, am I right?"

"Right," Melody and Chaz said together.

"Right," JD echoed. "So, here's the deal. You guys get to go back down until Monday. That way you can do the last two performances of the school play. The school will be informed that you're going back to your old school in Detroit. You can say good-

140

bye to Corky, pack it up, and wham, you're back here where you belong."

"It's really nice of you to give us time to go back and say good-bye," Melody said.

"Hey, I just thought of something," Chaz mused. "Why is it that when Melody and I kissed in her dressing room, we didn't go hurling off into space?"

"My guess is that Scarlett and her mom walked in just before you would have gone planet tripping," JD said. "In Latin we call it 'Lip-smackus Interruptus.'" He threw his head back and laughed. "Oh, in the words of Lavender, I just kill me! I have to remember to tell the Big Guy that one!"

"JD?" Chaz asked.

"Huh?" JD said, as soon as he could stop chuckling.

"I just thought of something else. Since we're going to be at Ground Zero on Monday," he said slowly, "there's something I would really, really like to do."

"What's that?" JD asked.

Chaz looked at Melody and smiled. "I would like to take Melody to her first art museum."

JD smiled. "You're all right, Chaz Denton," JD said with admiration.

"Right back 'atcha, JD," Chaz said with a grin, "right back 'atcha."

Twelve

"I think that's the last of the paperwork," the school secretary said, as Melody and Chaz signed some papers and dropped off the books that had been loaned to them. "Did you have a good time here at Whitmore?"

"It was great," Melody said.

"You were wonderful in *Bus Stop*," the secretary said. "And how about that Corky McGee!"

"Wasn't she great?" Chaz asked.

"I can't believe Scarlett Whitmore missed all three performances," the secretary said, shaking her head. "But Corky was incredible. No one around here will ever be able to look at her quite the same way!"

"Thanks for everything," Chaz said, and he and Melody slowly walked out of the office.

"Let's go by the gym," Melody said. "The cheerleaders are practicing."

They stood outside the gym and listened as the cheerleaders went through one of their new routines. Scarlett was there cheering with the others.

"Did you like being a cheerleader?" Chaz asked, as they watched.

"I loved it," Melody admitted softly. "Once play practice started I didn't really get to cheer anymore. But it was so much fun. And the other cheerleaders—besides Scarlett and Jennifer and Beth, that is—were really nice."

"You didn't get to do anything like that when you were alive, huh?" Chaz said.

"No," Melody said. "I missed so much school because of modeling jobs . . . everyone thinks that must have been so wonderful, but it wasn't."

Chaz didn't say anything, he just put his arm around her. Melody watched Scarlett as she did a cartwheel. "I let her down, didn't I, Chaz?" she said.

"Well, I guess it's like JD said," Chaz pointed out, "Scarlett wasn't ready to change."

"I want to try talking to her one more time," Melody said impetuously.

"But she snubbed you all day," Chaz said. "She acts as if you don't exist."

"Can you blame her?" Melody asked. "She thinks I stole her boyfriend."

"It's kind of hard for me to feel badly for Scarlett," Chaz said. "Look what she did! She ran out on the play. What would have happened if Corky hadn't stepped in? Then she told everyone she had stomach flu. But she's magically back at school on Monday. What a crock!"

"What did you expect her to say, 'I caught Melody kissing Chaz and I couldn't stand it?' "

"Honesty wouldn't kill her," Chaz mumbled.

At that moment Scarlett happened to turn in their direction, and she caught sight of the two of them peering in at her.

"Let's take five," Miss Sunder, the cheerleading coach, called out.

The girls scattered to get drinks or to use the ladies' room. Scarlett stayed where she was, but she turned away so that she didn't have to look at Melody.

"I'll be right back," Melody told Chaz.

"But—"

She didn't get to hear the rest of his protest as she hurried toward Scarlett.

"Scarlett?" Melody tapped her on the shoulder.

"What do you want?" Scarlett asked, as she slowly turned around.

"I wanted to talk to you," Melody said. "Today is my last day here—"

"Good riddance," Scarlett sneered.

"Scarlett, I want to apologize to you," Melody said in her breathy voice. "I should have told you that Chaz and I were involved back home—"

"That would have been nice," Scarlett said in bitter tones.

"I can't explain to you why we didn't tell you, or why we pretended we weren't a couple," Melody said. "I wish I could."

"The two of you were probably laughing at me—"

"No!" Melody protested. "We were never laughing at you!"

"—just like I always laughed at Corky McGee. Isn't that what you're thinking?"

"No," Melody said. "We never laughed at you. But the way you're hurting right now is probably a lot like Corky felt every time you and your friends hurt her."

Scarlett shook her hair out of her face. "What makes you so perfect, huh, Melody?"

"I'm not—"

"That's right, you're not," Scarlett shot back. "I'm sick of your lectures, okay? You're the kind of girl who lies to someone who was supposed to be her friend. You're the kind of girl who steals a guy behind another girl's back. So don't ever think you're better than me, because you're not."

"You're right," Melody said, a lump in her throat. "You're absolutely right."

They stared at each other for a moment.

"Well, I just wanted to say I'm sorry," Melody finally said. "I made a lot of mistakes. But I'll always remember you, Scarlett. And I'm sorry we couldn't have become better friends."

"Why should you always remember me?" Scarlett asked petulantly.

"Because you're special," Melody said softly. You'll always have been my very first mission, she thought to herself. I guess a Teen Angel never forgets that.

"I don't know why," Scarlett replied.

"Maybe you will," Melody said, "someday. But I hope it isn't for a really, really long time. See ya."

Melody got part way across the gym, when Scarlett called out to her. "Melody!"

She turned around.

Scarlett slowly walked over to her. "You know what you said to me that time? About Pickles? About why I love her so much?"

Melody nodded.

"Well, you were right," Scarlett said. "You were totally right."

Melody touched Scarlett's arm lightly. "Thanks for telling me," she said. "Good luck, Scarlett."

When Melody got back to where Chaz was waiting for her, she had a huge smile on her face.

"Don't tell me you two kissed and made up?" Chaz asked.

"No," Melody said thoughtfully. "But . . . it was a beginning, maybe." She looked at her watch. "We've got to go meet Corky at the theater. We're already five minutes late."

They headed for the west wing of the campus where the theater was located. Corky was sitting in the front row, staring up at the empty stage.

"Hi," Melody said. "Sorry we're late." She sat down next to Corky.

"I can't believe I was really up there and I was really good," Corky said.

"Believe it," Chaz said. "Everyone else in the whole school believes it."

"It was the greatest weekend of my life," Corky said. She turned to Melody. "It never would have happened without you."

"You're the one who did it, Corky," Melody said.

"No one ever believed in me before," Corky said. "Not even my parents, really. I mean, they're nice people and everything, but they're the kind of people who want to blend into the woodwork. They'd rather die than be in a play."

"So, where did you get your talent?" Chaz asked.

Corky shrugged. "When you spend a lot of time alone, you have a rich fantasy life." She turned to Melody again. "I can't believe you two are leaving . . ."

"I'll miss you," Melody said.

"I don't know if I can do it without you," Corky admitted in a scared voice.

"You can!" Melody insisted. "I know you can!" She searched her mind for the right thing to say, and then a pep talk that JD has once given her flew into her mind.

"I'm not telling you it's going to be easy," she said, unconsciously imitating JD. "But every time you get scared, I want you to remember that nothing worth doing comes easily, and no fight is won all at once, and . . . and yo, babe, you're worth it!"

Corky stared at her with incredulity. "Where did you get that from?"

"My . . . cousin!" Melody said brightly.

"He inspires her," Chaz agreed solemnly. "Of course, sometimes he does tend to sound like one of those really barfy inspirational posters . . ."

"Will you write to me?" Corky asked, as the three of them got up.

"I'll . . . try to stay in touch," Melody promised.

"I'll never forget you, Melody," Corky said.

"I won't forget you, either," Melody said.

The two girls hugged, then Corky quickly hugged Chaz.

"Go!" she cried, tears streaming down her face. "Do it fast so it won't hurt as much." She turned her back to them. "I'll just turn this way so I don't have to see you go."

"Bye, Corky," Melody said softly.

Hand in hand, Melody and Chaz walked up the aisle of the theater, down the hall, and out into the sunny, late afternoon air.

"I wonder what will happen to her," Melody asked, wiping a few tears from her own eyes.

"Maybe JD will let us look at her on the Future-scope sometime," Chaz said.

"Maybe," Melody said. She turned around and looked at Whitmore High. "Well, good-bye, high school."

"And hello, art museum," Chaz said. "You ready

for your first tour of the Whitney Museum, compliments of the traveling show at the Tennessee State Museum?''

"I'm ready," Melody said. "Just promise me you won't test me on any of this."

"I promise," Chaz said. He made a face.

"What is it?" Melody asked with concern.

"Well, I did get a note from Mr. Costello—"

"Our English teacher at Heaven High?" Melody asked, confused.

Chaz nodded. "When I got my assignment to join you, I told him I was hoping to take you to an art museum on Ground Zero. And . . . he said if we went we had to write a paper for class about it."

"He didn't!" Melody protested.

"He did," Chaz confirmed with a sigh. "Does it ruin the whole thing for you?"

"I refuse to let it," Melody decided. She looked up at the shining sun and felt its warmth on her cheeks. "Today we're here on Earth together. I don't know when we'll be back, or even if we'll ever get to be back here together. So . . . today is for just you and me."

Chaz turned to her and put his arms around her. "I love you, Mel," he said softly. "Up there and down here."

She raised her lips to his. And Melody knew that even if the passion of their kiss spun them out into the stratosphere, they would still come back down to Earth, for one last perfect day.

CHERIE BENNETT
BELIEVERS
F A N   C L U B

Hey, Readers! You asked for it, you've got it!

Join your Angel sisters from all over the world in the greatest fan club in the world...

CHERIE BENNETT BELIEVERS FAN CLUB!

Here's what you'll get:

★ a personally-autographed-to-you 8x10 glossy photograph of your favorite writer (I hope!).

★ a bio that answers all those weird questions you always wanted to know, like how Jeff and I met!

★ a three-times yearly newsletter, telling you everything that's going on in the worlds of your fave books, and me!

★ a personally-autographed-by-me membership card!

★ an awesome bumper sticker, a locker magnet, or a mini-notepad.

★ "Angel Sister" pen pal information that can hook you up with readers all over the world! Guys, too!

★ and much, much more!

So I say to you—don't delay! Fill out the request form here, clip it, and send it to the address below, and you'll be rushed fan club information and an enrollment form!

Yes! I'm a Cherie Bennett Believer! Cherie, send me information and an enrollment form so I can join the CHERIE BENNETT BELIEVERS FAN CLUB!

My Name _____

Address _____

Town _____

State/Province _____ Zip _____

Country _____

CHERIE BENNETT BELIEVERS FAN CLUB
P.O. Box 150236
Nashville, Tennessee 37215 USA

CBB 0296